Francis T. Furey, Francis d.-H. de Pressensé

Purcell's Manning Refuted

Life of Cardinal Manning with a Critical Examination of E. S. Purcell's Mistakes

Francis T. Furey, Francis d.-H. de Pressensé

Purcell's Manning Refuted

Life of Cardinal Manning with a Critical Examination of E. S. Purcell's Mistakes

ISBN/EAN: 9783337266509

Printed in Europe, USA, Canada, Australia, Japan

Cover: Foto ©Andreas Hilbeck / pixelio.de

More available books at **www.hansebooks.com**

PURCELL'S "MANNING" REFUTED.

LIFE

OF

CARDINAL MANNING

WITH

A CRITICAL EXAMINATION

OF

E. S. PURCELL'S MISTAKES.

BY

FRANCIS DE PRESSENSÉ

A FRENCH PROTESTANT.

TRANSLATED BY

FRANCIS T. FUREY, A. M.

———

PHILADELPHIA:
JOHN JOS. McVEY.
1897.

TRANSLATOR'S PREFACE.

No biography published in recent times has attracted so much attention as that of Cardinal Manning by E. S. Purcell. It has made a sensation such as no other work of its kind has caused, not even Froude's "Carlyle," with which it has so often been compared. Both are alike in the injudicious use each author has made of the materials at his disposal, but there the similarity ends; for while Froude succeeded in unintentionally ruining his hero's reputation, Purcell has only aided in making the great English Cardinal's nobility of character the better known through the almost innumerable refutations that he has called forth. And it is not only Catholic writers who have taken him to task; for Protestant defenders of Manning against his biographer have been even more numerous than they, and sometimes even warmer in their advocacy.

Nor have the assailants of Mr. Purcell because of what Mr. Stead has happily described as his "attempt on the life of Cardinal Manning," been confined to England or the English-speaking world. Deep interest in the subject has also been taken by continental writers, so deep indeed that at least in one instance it has been discussed far more elaborately than by any writer in

English. And this has been done, too, by a French-
man who is a Protestant, the son of a Calvinist minister. It is his work that is given here in an English
dress, with the hope that it may make the true Manning better known. No Catholic could write more
sympathetically of the subject than does M. de Pressensé, who, even in his comments on religious questions, says very little, almost nothing indeed, to which
a Catholic can take exception; while his book presents
the advantage of being not only a refutation, but at the
same time a biography as well. Perhaps the only
serious fault that one can find with him is his apparent
disparagement of Newman when he contrasts the characters of the two great princes of the Church. This,
however, does not detract from the value of his work,
which well deserves to retain a permanent place in
biographical literature.

CONTENTS.

(5)

PART FIRST.

INTRODUCTORY.

For the second and third parts of this work, written for a periodical publication,* no other ambition was entertained than to trace, in a necessarily imperfect abridgment, a slight sketch of one of the most exalted and most noble Christian personages that this century has presented to us. In reproducing them in a more durable form, without making any change in them, I am no doubt partly obeying too indulgent advice and solicitations too flattering; but I wanted especially not to leave unanswered certain criticisms occasioned by those modest articles.

If I had consulted only my own desire, and, I may add, my own interest, it would have been much better, in all probability, not to have sought to prolong the naturally ephemeral existence of a production altogether incidental. When one has long entertained the hope of one day writing the history of a great religious movement, the best means of furnishing a prelude to the carrying out of this project is not, undoubtedly, to offer

* They appeared originally in the *Revue des Deux Mondes* of May 1 and May 15, 1896, with the title: "Manning.—I. 'Les Années Protestantes.'—II. 'Les Années Catholiques.'"

(7)

to the public a hasty and incomplete sketch. No one realizes more than I do that defects and omissions disfigure the present study—imperfections perhaps necessarily entailed by the narrow compass or summary character of the narrative—and some also that it would have been easy for me to avoid. I do not pretend to give here a full-length portrait of Cardinal Manning, nor especially a portrait that is worthy in every respect of that great original. Very much less have I entertained the illusion of presenting an account, or even an outline, of the origin and progress of Anglo-Catholicism.

In this essay, as in all those of a biographical nature, there is, if I may venture to say so, at the same time more and less than in a chapter of history—less, because there is question only of a single individual and not of a great party or rather of a whole generation; more, nevertheless, because there is nothing like the infinite complexity and inexhaustible wealth of a man's soul, and because that is precisely what it has been proposed to depict. The very kindly feelings that have been aroused by the publication of these pages, and that have encouraged me, perhaps imprudently, to bring them out in a new form, are, I feel certain, due entirely to whatever there is in Cardinal Manning's personality that is human, pathetic, emotional and dramatic. As regards the occasional severe criticisms and bitter rebukes that have been unsparingly heaped upon me, they have been evidently due especially to my ability being too obviously insufficient for me to do full justice to this great subject. I would not dare to assert, however, that there are not in them traces of that narrow-

ness of mind and of heart, and of those sectarian prejudices, which seem to me to be much more out of place
here than anywhere else.

Assuredly, in paying a homage that I wanted to
make as striking as possible to one of the men who,
having gone out from the pale of Protestantism, have
contributed most to the restoration of Catholicism as a
spiritual power and to the triumph of the doctrines
called Ultramontane, I was not ignorant either of what
I was doing or of what I ought to expect. Nothing
could appear more natural to me, more legitimate even,
than the surprise or even irritation of certain minds.
I had foreseen certain objections, nay, even certain protests in the name of the principles of the Reformation.

If a Protestant critic, without entering into a detailed
examination of the facts on which I thought I could
base my admiration, my respect, my veneration for
Cardinal Manning, had remained satisfied with asking
me, by way of preliminary inquiry, how I thought of
reconciling this condition of soul with the profession of
Protestantism; if another, giving an interpretation different from mine to the known documents or appealing
to new ones, had disputed, with the evidence in hand,
my method of relating and passing judgment upon the
events of Manning's inner and outer life; if a third,
setting the biography aside altogether, had placed side
by side the principles that are explicitly or implicitly
laid down in these pages, the prejudices that they betray, the sympathies or antipathies that they unveil,
the judgments that they pass on the men and things of
both denominations, in order to discuss and refute them;

if either, in fine, bringing all these data together, drawing their logical conclusions from these premises, had been pleased to contrast with and oppose to the positive assertions and involuntary avowals that he thought he found in my articles, in regard to my opinions on the most serious subjects, what he thought he knew of my acknowledged convictions or even of my inmost feeling, I might have been able to regret certain acts of injustice, to deplore certain failures in tact, to dispute certain deductions, to combat certain arguments, nay even to disallow certain jurisdictions; it would have been impossible for me to complain of a mode of controversy so respectful of an adversary's conscience.

There might have been error on one side or on the other,—perhaps on both at one and the same time; what would have been on neither would be the spirit of contention and quibbling, the implicit assertion of moral superiority, the sickly need of excommunication. God forbid that I be such an ingrate as to pretend that I have met with none but ill-natured disputants. How shall I forget the exquisite delicacy, the discreet solicitude of men in whom I was accustomed to venerate authentic witnesses in favor of living Christianity, and who, compelled by their conscience to point out errors, in their estimation fatal, have done so with a moderation, a patience, a breadth, a charity in a word, for which I am ever grateful to them? I could name publicists, religious writers, ever so far from approving of my judgments, who, however, have not thought it their duty—or their right—to hurl the thunderbolts of the major excommunication, to condemn in a lump and without appeal, to feign superior intelligence on questions of fact or of persons, in which the elements of an independent opinion were wanting to them; in fine, to give to the public, as news worthy of credence, gratuitous inventions springing from their brain and from it only.

Articles like that of the *Journal Religieux de la Suisse Romande* show clearly that there is a method of controversy in which fidelity most uncompromising to the principles of Protestantism by no means excludes Christian charity. There is, then, a means of speaking one's thoughts frankly, but also with perfect courtesy. It is not necessary, then, that in such a case discussion should degenerate, in its subordinate development, into a pitiful homily or a virulent demand. I know that in this respect there is in him who has signed these lines an hereditary tradition of fairness, civility and justice; we cannot require such generous methods of every one.

Why should it be, however, that I find myself compelled to refer to attacks directed in so different a spirit? One begins by hiding his face at the mere spectacle of the scandal given by a Protestant by birth speaking sympathetically, admiringly, of a pervert from Protestantism. He is indignant at the effrontery of a writer who dares to find fault with the manner of writing history adopted by Mr. Purcell, who is suddenly promoted to the rank of a serious author drawing upon original sources. According to him, there is intolerable lack of regard for consistency and even of good faith in taking from the book of Cardinal Manning's self-

appointed biographer the proofs of the innumerable
errors of fact and of the incomparably more gross and
more culpable errors of judgment committed by this
singular depictor, who seems to have no dearer pleasure
than to disfigure the features and to demean the expression of his subject.

Critics who probably have not taken the trouble to
read, and especially to study minutely the sixteen
hundred pages of Mr. Purcell's massive work, do not
admit that one has the right to pass severe judgment
on a book in which a systematic malevolence towards
one of the great men of modern Catholicism has served
with them as a sufficient recommendation.   Mr. Purcell's two volumes are full of insinuations, accusations
and condemnations against Cardinal Manning; that suffices: they are the work of a master hand; they must be
accepted as gospel truth, and to point out gross errors,
monstrous contradictions, stupefying evidences of ignorance, constant falsification of dates, inaccurate quotations, mutilated documents, disorder in thought,
vulgarity in style, and, worse than all that, a spirit of
disparagement and of calumny that make of this work
a sad monument of all that a biography worthy of this
name ought not to be, is to expose oneself to being
taxed with prejudice in favor of the Church of Rome
and with treason against the Reformation.

But this is not all. Such a defender of Protestant
orthodoxy goes farther. Not satisfied with rummaging
with a far from light hand in the most secret and most
sacred recesses of a man's conscience, our journalist
arrogates to himself the attributes of a prophet. Offici-

ally, as if he could have no doubt of it, or rather as if
he had received an express mandate about it, he an-
nounces as an accomplished fact a conversion or an
abjuration, which is quite simply the logical conclusion
which it has pleased him to draw from the premises
that he has laid down. He is so sure of his fact that
he himself comments on the news that he has just
given, and in which he would have indeed liked, as he
declares in no uncertain terms, to place no confidence.

And then it is a little play that begins.

The information thus put in circulation is taken up
by the myriad echoes of publicity. After the religious
it is the turn of the secular, and then even of the boule-
vard press. Comments go their way. Each new stage
in the flight of this canard gives it an increase of vi-
tality. Ere long, those even who have taken the liberty of thus playing with your name have a grievance
against you. Of their certain knowledge and full
power it has pleased them to attribute to you an act
too important and touching too closely on the domain
of conscience for it not to have been necessary to verify
its authenticity, twice rather than once, before launch-
ing the assertion of it. They have a grudge against you
for the silence that you keep. They reproach you
with lack of respect for the public if you decline the
arbitrary jurisdiction of the third or of the fourth.
They summon you to answer questions that they have
not the right to put to you. If you do not consent to
send back the ball they will do you up handsomely.
Should you have the weakness to entertain any out-of-
date prejudice against the violation of a certain modesty

of soul; should you positively refuse to bring out into
the broad daylight of publicity, not your actions, your
words, or your very thoughts, but the innermost conflict and most secret anguish of your soul, they will
show you clearly that you are wrong and that the press
has the right to learn everything, or rather, to know
everything.

Thus old-time methods are perpetuated while adapt-
ing themselves to the mildness of our present manners.
Thank God, there is no longer a tribunal of the Inquisi-
tion; but are we quite sure that some of its methods do
not survive and that they are not occasionally applied
in the name and to the advantage of the religion of free
examination, of individualism and of freedom of conscience? Nor is it amiss to note that there is something rather pointed in seeing oneself excommunicated
by Geneva—I mean, put outside the communion of the
visible Church by its champions by reason of their
office, under the pretext of a too obvious predilection
for the visible Church. The paradox would be quite
agreeable if there was question here only of making
merry over the inconsistencies of one's judges.

Unfortunately, these controversies do not fail to have
their echo outside, in many upright hearts and simple
minds. An equanimity of soul bordering very closely
on the indifference of egoism would be necessary in
order to have recourse against all this noise only to absolute silence. By saying nothing one also risks becoming an object of scandal. This is why I thought it
my duty to repel here attacks to which, if there was
question only of myself, I would not perhaps have

thought of answering. Certainly, I have taken no account of those anonymous enthusiasts of a *pure and spotless religion* who, forgetting to attach their signatures, have leveled at me a broadside of pious insults. With these anonymous writers I certainly do not confound the champions of the Gospel who arrogate to themselves the right of throwing your most sacred memories in your face and of bringing your filial affection into question because of differences of opinion; but I will be allowed to answer them with some emotion.

In truth, what then do they know of the inheritance of true liberalism, of breadth of view in connection with faith, left to me by my father, Edmond de Pressensé—they who are pleased to invoke and to use against me the memory of him who was formerly called the Protestant Montalembert? Assuredly I know better than they the inviolable and inflexible fidelity that he, until the end, devoted to the Church of his choice—how much that Christianity which upheld him in a cruel agony of eighteen months was thoroughly penetrated with the spirit of individualistic Protestantism—to what point, in those last months in which he was called upon to live what he had believed the principles of his preferred master, Alexandre Vinet, assumed in his estimation a degree of fresh evidence—with what severity even he believed he ought to judge certain recent developments of Catholicism.

Never did the idea even occur to me of invoking certain phrases inadvertently improvised by him, which others have not had the same scruples about using and which seemed to tend to predicting the

failure of the Reformation in France.   I do not dream
of recalling the virulent attacks occasioned against the
intrepid champion of liberty of conscience by the energy
of his attitude in the Senate against anti-clerical
tyranny, with its Article 7, its expulsions of the members of religious orders, its brutal suppression of the
budget of worship, and its watchword: *Let the pastors
take bags on their backs!* All the pretension I make—
and on this point, I confess, I admit neither dispute
nor reply—is that I be indeed allowed to derive my inspiration, if not from some or from all of my father's
opinions, at least from their spirit itself, in proportion
as I think I understand it.   Let me be allowed to invoke one of the noblest and most generous recommendations that he bequeathed to his people, and by which
he warned them never to allow a sentiment due to his
memory to be used against an idea adopted for sufficient reasons.

As long as I proceed according to the dictates of my
conscience; as long as the opinions, whether popular or
unpopular, that I embrace are imposed upon me by
their apparent conformity with truth and by it only; as
long as the voice that I strive to listen to and to follow
is that of Christ, it will be impossible for me to attach
a tragic importance to divergences of views necessarily
of secondary consideration.   The agreement that, after
all, is alone important, is not perhaps even that which
is produced on the fundamental points of thought: it is
the harmony of souls, it is the ear inclined and the
spirit opened in the direction of Revelation.   The rest
could not be of capital importance; and a very strange

conception of filial devotion is necessary in order to make the duty of thinking in the same way about the seat of authority and about the apostolical succession enter into it.

Truly, these personalities are the fruit of a zeal whose source I know how to respect, just as I could not have a grudge against those good people who have signified to me their displeasure at seeing me pass a favorable judgment on an "agent of Rome," who have reproached me with my ignorance by revealing to me that *Protestant peoples are infinitely more prosperous than Catholic peoples,* and who have recommended me to read a book on the conflicts between science and faith, in which Catholicism is directly attacked with arguments taken from the arsenal of popular free-thought and which would leave nothing of Christianity standing. It suffices that upright souls, those consciences in the pure mirror of which is reflected the religion of Christ, have been troubled, disturbed, saddened, so that there be occasion to offer all the explanations compatible with the rights of truth.

Since none of those in whose good faith I sincerely believe have been scandalized at the manner in which I have treated the author of the "Life of Cardinal Manning" and his work, however strange their interest in such a client may seem to be, I owe them a justification of my opinion of Mr. Purcell and his book, more ample than that of my articles. Since others have been astonished at the very choice of this subject and at seeing a writer who, in any case, should not be accused of having been brought up in the sacristy, treat

2

Manning's personality with such tender respect, I wish
to state briefly the reasons for this effort.

Since several of my critics, in fine, have without
circumlocution raised the question of my own religious
convictions; since they have striven with all their might
either to set me in contradiction with myself or to convince me of some indefinable Catholicizing dilettantism,
or to compel me at once and already to complete the
evolution whose circuit they have calculated for me
and to justify the syllogism that they have constructed
in my behalf, by admitting like them the necessity of
one of those acts on which one does not go back and by
completing my abjuration, I owe it to them, I owe it
to myself, to trace as faithfully as possible the condition of soul that gave rise to these articles—and until
now to these only.

I.

Before touching on any other point, it is proper, then,
that I explain myself in regard to the case of Mr. Purcell, the author of the two massive volumes that contain
the life of Manning, and that have served as the occasion and the theme of my study. The judgment that
I felt myself obliged to pass on him in the *Revue des
Deux Mondes*, and which I think I ought to keep un-
altered in this volume, is marked with much severity
and at the same time differs so completely from that of
certain of my critics that I would expose myself to all
the severity of the most pitiless judgment if I did not
try to give a serious reason for it. In the brief summary to which I have been compelled to confine my-

self, I was prevented from entering into the details of this examination; I had to remain satisfied with a summary description of Mr. Purcell's manner of writing history, and to proceed on the line of assertions, instead of following the slow course of a regular demonstration.

Several of my censors have shown the greatest ill-will against me on this account. They would, I imagine, have been somewhat embarrassed in justifying the sympathetic, nay, almost tender interest that Mr. Purcell has awakened in them. To men ill-disposed towards Manning it was a real piece of good fortune to find a biographer, Catholic in religion, who announced himself as authorized and almost as official, who had unquestionably drawn upon the most authentic sources, who undoubtedly produced a most formidable array of new documents, and who, while incessantly protesting his love and respect for his hero, poured out floods of discredit and shame upon him, by his narratives, by his judgments, by his accusations, and even by his praises. On the contrary, is it not intolerable that a writer whose antecedents scarcely admit of his discarding impartiality *a priori*, and who can hardly be accused of obeying preconceived sympathies, should turn up to spoil everything?

It would have been difficult to make a grievance against me of my not having espoused, with my eyes shut, the assertions of the so-called Catholic historian; of my not wanting either to accept his facts without verification, or to endorse his judgments without reserve. What they have not failed to blame severely was either the effrontery of pretending to point out the way to my master or the indecency of borrowing the chief materials of my study from a book that I treated so rudely. A strange reproach, forsooth, as if there was the least logical contradiction, or the slightest moral indelicacy, in making use of documents that one has previously sifted with criticism, in confronting an author with himself before drawing upon him and of asking himself to supply the means of rectifying or refuting him.

Moreover, by no means is there question of an isolated text. Mr. Purcell's biography has merely had to take its place in the list of the already numerous works, the titles of the chief of which I gave at the head of my first article. Manning himself had already produced a rather copious literature. It is not even one of the slightest grievances to be alleged against this surprising biographer that he has treated with extraordinary disdain as well the authors who had preceded him as the works of Manning himself. An historian who does not find a passage worth borrowing in Mr. Hutton's little volume or in the brief and substantial pamphlet in which Dr. Gasquet has given an admirable sketch of Cardinal Manning's spiritual expression—a writer who does not look for a single point of information in the sermons, prefaces, and innumerable other productions that came from the Archbishop of Westminster's pen during sixty years' activity, betrays a singular lack of preparation for his task.

Fortunate had it been if he had committed only this grave sin of omission! Mr. Purcell will not have contracted a debt of gratitude towards his champions: it is they who compel us to produce the proofs of our accusations and to reveal to the public what is covered by and on what rest the so-called judge's pretended decrees on Cardinal Manning. Let us speak in the first place of the spirit in which Mr. Purcell approached his task. To a biographer, he himself very justly says, his hero ought to be an object of special, of supreme interest, and, we will add, of respectful sympathy. Without this disposition it would be better to leave the carrying out of the mission to some one else than to take it upon oneself. Well! I make bold to assert that that is precisely the feeling in which Mr. Purcell is most obviously lacking.

Whether he entertained an old-time unfavorable prejudice against Manning, or rather belongs to that category of minds that are incapable of feeling for a long time a real admiration for any one whomsoever, and that speedily grow weary, in studying or in relating his life, of calling Aristides the Just, at every instant he betrays an instinctive malevolence, one might almost say a preconceived hostility which only grows and is embellished at every step, against the Archbishop of Westminster. I cannot think of citing all the passages in which this state of soul breaks out; some typical examples will suffice to give an idea of it.

Even before having under consideration, no longer a fully developed boy, but a character already formed, he cannot help attributing the most lamentable pettiness to Manning. At school, he represents him as never speaking of others (in letters or in his diary), but from compensation, ever ready to converse minutely

and abundantly of himself (Vol. I, p. 18). At the
University, he attributes to him, with a vanity extend-
ing even to his toilet, an egotism, an exaggerated consciousness of himself, which, according to our author,
was to remain attached to him, like a Nessus tunic,
until the end of his life (ib., p. 30). Led to note that
at this date Manning is less concerned with religious
questions than with politics, he says amiably that the
young man could speak only of the subjects that
brought him an audience hanging on his lips (ib., p. 61).
He writes, without seeming to suspect the wrong that
such an assertion, if it were true, would do to him who
is its object, that fortune, that anti-spiritual divinity,
in whose presence Manning had assumed the habit of
bowing, asked its faithful adorer for one homage, one
sacrifice more (ib., p. 195). He speaks, in a passing
way, as of the most natural thing in the world, of the
habit, partly congenital, partly acquired by Manning,
of never committing himself to an unpopular movement
and of never taking position on the side of an unfortunate cause (ib., p. 204). Farther on he represents
Manning as a man ready to recede from no sacrifice of
friendship when there was question of the Church or of
his personal interest (ib., p. 244).

In a truly typical passage he paints this new Machia-
velli, this Anglican Jesuit, much more concerned with
serving his party *in the palaces* than *in the universities;*
infinitely less anxious to study the *subtleties of theology,*
the *Fathers of the Church* and *Catholic antiquity* than to
follow the *intrigues of Parliament and of the Court;* far
from deeply absorbed in the publication of "Tract

No. 90," the storm that it let loose, the reawakening of Anglo-Catholicism of which it was the occasion, but all engrossed *in the antechamber rumors of Downing street* (*ib.*, p. 265). To him Manning is the *adorer of the rising sun*, the *enemy of unpopular minorities*, the *born deserter of condemned causes*.

It seems to me that it suffices to reproduce these monstrous passages in order to place their author in a strange embarrassment. If these references be correct, how did Mr. Purcell come to entertain the idea of writing the life of this courtier of fortune, of this ambitious man, of this intriguing ecclesiastic? How especially did he think he could make a hero and a saint of him? By what marvelous sleight-of-hand did he hope to reconcile these judgments, hurled as he went along, with the final formula of canonization that crowns his work? I leave to Mr. Purcell the task of reconciling these contradictions. For my part, it suffices for me to place these indescribable calumnies side by side with the facts—I mean those very facts that are stated by our author and in the documents that he had at his disposal and that he has communicated to us. The reader will undoubtedly find the expression not too strong when he will have followed me into one or two of these proofs.

To begin, let us take Manning's entrance into orders. For telling us of this important event Mr. Purcell had before him a certain number of documents which he has published in the strange manner that is familiar to him, as I will show farther on, but which, in fine, he has laid before our eyes. The materials consisted of

three autobiographical notes, drawn up by the Cardinal
some fifty years after the date of the facts to which they
refer; letters and fragments of letters, some of them, on
the contrary, written as early as 1832, especially those
to his mother and to Mr. Twistleton, a friend of his
when a young man. It is shown as clear as day from
these documents that Manning, whether at that very
period or half a century later, was absolutely convinced
that he ought to obey a vocation from on high, an appeal, as he himself said, from God *ad veritatem et ad
ipsum.* All the testimonies point to this meaning; there
is not the shadow of a single one of them with an opposite sense: one might think that Mr. Purcell would
feel bound to follow this version, the only authentic
one.

This would come from knowing him imperfectly, indeed. He insinuates that Manning's vocation was
most probably the fruit of an illusion; that the young
clergyman was himself duped if he thought he was
obeying any other considerations than purely mundane
motives, and that in reality he felt none of the religious
emotions whose effect on his soul he pointed out later
on. That is clear speaking. One would only like to
know on what all this scaffolding of hypotheses rests
and where are the documents that entitle our author
thus to belie his hero to his face. Documents! there
are none. Mr. Purcell has simply judged as improbable and absurd a *motive as strange and as extraordinary*
as a divine vocation. Forgetting the two absolutely
contemporary letters that he himself has published and
that confirm on every point the later version of the

diary, he holds that the Cardinal, in time, had lost the exact recollection of the manner in which things had happened and had somewhat embellished his story. Moreover, if this reasoning does not convince the reader, he has an argument in reserve that he deems irresistible: if Manning, he says, had really heard this appeal, he would without fail have communicated it to his confidant, his daily correspondent, his brother-in-law, Mr. John Anderdon. Now, he did not do so: he did not, then, obey this supernatural impulse.

The syllogism is correct. Mr. Purcell's logic is faultless, with the unfortunate exception that his minor is false. Manning had precisely made known to his brother-in-law the feelings with which he was animated. There is in existence a copy of his letters in two small books that escaped Mr. Purcell. Dr. Gasquet, who married a niece of the Cardinal's, had quoted from them on pages 10 and 11 of his brief pamphlet published in 1895, two extracts that finally dispose of all of Mr. Purcell's quibbles. The author of the pretended authorized biography, if he had deigned to cast his eyes on this modest and admirable little work, would have found in it not only information such as this, drawn from a proper source, but also a luminous and delicate analysis of Cardinal Manning's spiritual character. *Ab uno disce omnes.* Such is the spirit with which the so-called official biographer approached his task!

It is this same singular need of blackening that guided him in his manner of relating and of judging another episode. There is question of Manning's re-

fusal, in 1846, of the place of sub-chaplain to the Queen
that was offered to him in consequence of the promotion of his brother-in-law, Samuel Wilberforce, to the
episcopate.   This post was the first step in the ladder
of honors.   It would have brought Manning close to
the Court, it would have facilitated for him that rapid
advancement which everybody prognosticated for him,
and which would have enticed him rather keenly, if he
had been the ambitious man of whom his enemies
speak—and along with them his biographer.   Well!
his diary of that period shows him to us, after a
week's reflection, as meeting that offer with a deliberate
refusal, and giving as the reason for it the obligation of
his parish care of souls, the necessity of mortifying
himself interiorly and the higher interest of his own
soul.   "To learn to say no," he wrote in these pages
made for himself only, "to disappoint myself, to choose
the harder part, to resist my own inclination, to prefer
that people think less well of me, to receive less of the
gifts of this world, that could not be an error: that too
closely resembles the cross.   Oh! humility, nothing but
humility! may God grant it to me!"   Will any one believe it?   It was after having had this passage before
his eyes, it was after having reproduced both the decision and its motives, that Mr. Purcell took upon himself to give to Manning lessons in renunciation and
humility.   He taxes him unsparingly with ambition
and worldliness.   He represents him as having regrets
that he is pleased to attribute *to remorse or to the restless-
ness of his temperament, or to both these causes at one and
the same time.*

Strange, nevertheless, as this manner of writing history may be, side by side with the original documents and in spite of them, so far, comparatively, it is only trifles. Mr. Purcell did not stop at so favorable a point. He unqualifiedly accuses Manning of having adopted an attitude and language bearing the ear-marks of duplicity from 1846 to 1851; of having for six years concealed from his Church, and from his best friends, the condition of his soul and his most secret feelings; of having, in a word, covered with the veil of an odious hypocrisy the great spiritual work that was to lead him to the Catholic Church. If this reproach be well-founded, it is not only this period of Manning's life that is tarnished and dishonored by it; it is his whole existence, his whole character, his whole being, that are stained by the most repugnant duplicity. His dearest convictions, his charity, his holiness even, have their roots in lying. The vain undertaking of proposing to the admiration of men a master in the perfidious art of using words with double meanings and of double-dealing acts must be abandoned. One does not understand why Mr. Purcell wasted his time in raising a monument to him of whom he formed such an idea. This contradiction is surprising. How is it, besides, that the author of this accusation feels its gravity so little that in a certain sense he launches it in passing, without unfolding all its consequences? Thank Heaven, here again the proofs are totally wanting, or rather all of them agree in refuting this calumny.

Let us listen to a justly respected periodical, edited in an entirely Anglican spirit, far from prejudiced in favor of perverts from the national Church, the *Spectator* (February 8, 1896): "In the private diaries and letters purporting to give what Mr. Purcell calls the 'inner man,' who doubted the validity of the Anglican position from 1846 to 1850, we find likewise expressed his suspicion that the doubt may be due to delusion. This being so, he declares it to be his duty to speak hopefully of the English Church and not to unsettle others in their allegiance to it. And in the letters cited in the same chapter as giving the 'outer man,' or the 'public voice,' we do *not* find assertions inconsistent with private doubts of the Anglican position; but rather a line of argument which urges the duty of remaining in the Anglican Communion in spite of personal doubts."

The case could not be better expressed, and this testimony of a competent and impartial critic will no doubt balance in the reader's mind the imputations dictated to a self-styled friend by a malevolent prejudice and an incredible confusion of thoughts. To the *Spectator*, as well as to me, Manning's honesty was absolute during that long and difficult and painful period when it was hardly possible for him to put into his language and his attitude more unity than there was in the conceptions of his inner consciousness.

Certainly I will not be required to examine with a magnifying glass the singular tissue of errors and sophisms on which Mr. Purcell bases his words. Let us remain satisfied with pointing out, in an argumentation in which dates are naturally of capital importance, the incurable levity with which Mr. Purcell assigns on a single page, a few lines apart, two different years,

1847 and 1849, to a letter which, a few pages further on, he again dates otherwise, and whose meaning, moreover, he totally distorts to the advantage of his cause. Has he at least adopted a more conscientious method when he has come to the years of Manning's life as a Catholic, that is to say, to the portion of his career for which one can and ought to suppose that he has more sympathy and is better equipped? He has taken care not to do so. It is always the same morbid need of soiling his hero that dominates in him. In the affair of Cardinal Wiseman's coadjutor *cum jure successionis*, one would say, if he is to be heeded, that Manning interfered in it, *proprio motu*, that it was he who stirred up the war and drove it to extremes, and that he followed it out for personal ends. How was it that our author, in the entirely disproportioned space, moreover, of nearly two hundred pages of his second volume that he has given to that episode at the risk of outrageously falsifying the true character of two episcopates, did not find room to say that Manning had been officially commissioned by his archbishop to attend to this affair at the court of Rome, that he was acting in accordance with hierarchical obedience, and that he could not do otherwise?

What an odious falsification it is to represent the correspondence between Manning and Mgr. George Talbot as a sort of intrigue plotted by an ambitious man, desirous of reaching the ear of the Holy Father, and far from scrupulous as to the choice of means! Was Mr. Purcell aware, yes or no, that the private chamberlain was the regular, recognized, normal organ of communications that had not to pass through the college of the Propaganda; that he was Cardinal Wiseman's accredited agent at the court of Rome, and that Manning, in writing to him, did nothing but obey and follow the example of all his colleagues of the archiepiscopal staff? These are very strange, very suspicious acts of forgetfulness. It is true that they fade before the guilty free-and-easy way in which the so-called authorized biographer has cast before the public the confidential notes of a secret correspondence, has scandalized some and hurt others by reviving old quarrels, and has maliciously isolated Manning's letters alone.

As he found time to write so copiously the history of this conflict, and yet did not feel bound to expatiate on Manning's diocesan activity, on his spiritual and charitable works, on his preaching, on his directing of consciences, on his books and on his works, he should have at least completed his picture by tracing the final peace-making. Does a man write with the impartiality of an historian, to say nothing of the good-will of a friend, when he relates lengthily the quarrels between Manning and Canon Maguire, their pointed words, their sometimes hostile proceedings, and yet says nothing of their reconciliation, of that long malady during which the Archbishop came every day to visit his old adversary, who exclaimed from his death-bed: "Your steps on the stairway have been music in my ears?" After having related Wiseman's painful conflict with his coadjutor, Errington, was it, then, not necessary also to describe the noble serenity of the submission

with which the former Archbishop of Trebizond retired
into a small country parish and forgot, in the care of
souls in that remote villlage, the greatness that came
near being his own? There is as much bad faith in
being silent on fine traits of this sort as there would be
in a wholesale inventing of regrettable incidents.

How, in fine, are we to qualify the inspiration that
presided over the interminable recital of the misunderstandings between Newman and Manning? Mr. Purcell, from one end to the other, exalts him whose life he
is not writing and lowers him who is regarded as his
hero. His partiality breaks out even so strongly that
it is its own antidote. He does not know how to see a
wrong in the Edgbaston Oratorian, nor a meritorious
act in the Archbishop of Westminster. Here, fortunately, the matter too far surpasses the imperturbably
judicial mediocrity of our historian. It is too evidently
not in his province to harmonize such differences—

Tantas componere lites.

Documents abound. He has added quite a cargo of
them to those that we already possessed. I am sure
that the competent public will know how to discern the
truth; that they will extricate, not without deploring
them, the causes of this regrettable misunderstanding;
that they will take account of the circumstances, of the
personalities and of the surroundings, and that they
will by no means subscribe to the unjust condemnation
formulated against Manning by a man as far from capable of penetrating his soul and of understanding his
nature as of entering into Newman's inner life.

The evil is not perhaps very great, even though temporary or passing critics, ever on the watch for some happy chance that dispenses them from reading a work before giving an account of it, have made the utmost use of this intermediary, and though partisans ever greedy for scandals in a rival denomination have moralized as best they could on that edifying spectacle of the quarrel between the two restorers of English Catholicism. If the public had not taken literally the noisy claims by which Mr. Purcell and his friends had announced the publication of his book:

Nescio quid majus nascitur Iliade !

if they had not unaffectedly put faith in our author's somewhat too advantageous pretentions, all these perfidies would have scarcely any importance.

Unfortunately, people in general are still ignorant of the fact that, far from being chosen by Cardinal Manning to write his life, Mr. Purcell obtained from that ever charitable prelate an authorization that was only a sort of delicately veiled assistance, because he had made a poor mouth, because there was question of relieving him from desperate straits, and because he had declared that he would find a gold mine in the publication of a book of this sort. People will be astonished that Mr. Purcell, who has seen fit to make room for so many suspicious anecdotes, did not spare two or three lines to pay homage to this generosity. People will be still more astonished that, treated with such great kindness, but without the least familiarity, by the Cardinal, he knew how to pose as his hero's confidential intimate

friend.   Surprise will touch very close on another feeling when people will learn that, instead of having had
innumerable conversations, and the prolonged relations
that seem to be implied by his narrative, with the Cardinal's then only surviving sister, Mrs. Austin, he had
in reality only seen her *but once* for an hour or two, and
then this lady was already far advanced in years.   I
set aside the question of propriety, or rather of delicacy
and honor, raised by the singular treatment of Manning
by a writer to whom he had opened the treasures of his
heart and of his memory.   It will suffice for me to remark that no more in this chapter than in the others is
Mr. Purcell worthy of implicit confidence.   Truly I am
happy to think that, on this point as on so many
others, the radical inaccuracy of his assertions pertains,
not to the deliberate purpose of deceiving, but to a con-
stitutional incapacity for telling the truth.

For the faculty of falling into error is really phenom-
enal in Mr. Purcell.   One might say without exaggeration that it is in spite of him and by mere chance that
he sometimes finds the truth.   He begins by making a
mistake of a year in the date of Manning's birth, and
that voluntarily, in opposition to all the previous testimonies and existing titles.   In his picture of the University of Oxford he commits a series of gross errors
from which the slightest glance at a Calendar would
have saved him.   To him the question of Catholic
Emancipation, settled in 1829 by Sir Robert Peel and
Wellington, is still under consideration three years
later.   He confounds epochs that are most distinct from
one another to the extent of giving Pusey's name to the

3

Oxford movement at a date when the Regius Professor
of Hebrew had not yet given public adhesion to Tractarianism.   I could indefinitely multiply these proofs
of ignorance and levity that cannot fail to cause confusion.

Perhaps some one will plead extenuating circumstances for what bears on the Anglican period of Manning's life.   After all, Mr. Purcell is a Catholic by
birth, and though he should have conscientiously prepared himself for speaking of things and people whom
he did not know at first hand, one may use indulgence
towards him in this domain.   But what are we to say
of the still more monstrous errors that he commits
when he has approached the Catholic period of the
Archbishop of Westminster's life, and when he moves
on ground that ought to be familiar to him?   Here I
will confine myself to pointing out a single error, but I
think that after having measured it there will not be
found many people of good faith who will still defend
Mr. Purcell's competence.

Open the second volume of this monumental work,
at page 532.   The very title of this nineteenth chapter,
of itself alone, has something calculated to plunge you
into a condition of surprise: *The second English cardinal
since the Reformation*, is the title that our author gives to
the section of his book in which he relates Manning's
promotion to the Roman purple.   Thus to him the
English cardinals who received the hat since 1540,
Pole, Allen, Weld, Norris, Howard, York, Acton, etc.,
have no reality, and there was no English prince of
the Church before Manning but Wiseman.

Let us continue. Mr. Purcell asks how it happens that the titles of the great champion of Infallibility at the Vatican Council could have remained unknown for such a long time. Had he been forgotten in the surroundings of Pius IX? Had he stirred up irreconcilable opposition in the Sacred College? It is to this last hypothesis that our historian has recourse, and he writes the following lines, whose savor I would reproach myself for spoiling by any commentary whatever: "[Pius IX] had not forgotten Archbishop Manning. He had proposed, in the first or second year after the Council, his name for election to the Sacred College. But the Cardinals, acting within their right, had declined to elect him. Three years later, after the death of Cardinal Barnabò, Prefect of Propaganda, no friend of Manning's, the Pope again proposed him. It is the custom of the College of Cardinals to elect unanimously a candidate proposed for the second time, since they regard it as an expression of the Pope's deliberate wish and determination. Accordingly, at the Consistory held on the 15th of March, 1875, Archbishop Manning was admitted by an unanimous vote into the College of Cardinals."

It would diminish the value of this incomparable pearl to insist too much upon it. Thus, to Mr. Purcell, a Catholic historian, the Sacred College is recruited by coöptation, and the part of the Sovereign Pontiff is confined to proposing candidates whom the cardinals reject or accept at their pleasure. One should not require a very exact knowledge of history nor a very strict method from a man who forms such ideas of the most eminent institutions of his own Church.

And so, indeed, there is nothing like the disorder, or rather chaos, of Mr. Purcell's mind. Having at his disposal a mass of original documents of different origin and dates, he should have begun by classifying them, dividing them between the series of contemporary pieces and that of retrospective writings, according to chronological order; instead of that, he has in some way thrown them in his reader's face. Constantly a letter is found ten pages after what it should have preceded. Another re-appears three times with slight alterations in the text under three different dates. He cuts up into the smallest fragments the documents he makes use of, and he takes pleasure in scattering these *membra disjecta*. His own narrative is no less confused. He goes back twice, three times, nay oftener, over the same subject, resumes, stops short, contradicts himself, forgets what he has just said.

Such is the author whom certain critics, seized with superstitious respect, have wanted to dub an infallible historian. Such is the writer whom certain persons whom I strongly suspect—and it is almost an extenuating circumstance—of not having read him, and have wished to impute to me as a crime my having pronounced against him as a witness and as a judge. Such is the incomparable master at whose feet one should have sat down and repeated with the docility of a child, not only his calumnies against the dead, but even his marvelous discoveries in modern history. I make bold to hope that after a little demonstration which imprudent friends have made necessary, admirers will no longer be found so blinded by the spirit of sectarianism as to persist in confidently invoking Mr. Purcell's testimony, were it against the hero of his biography.

II.

I need hardly say that it is not, however, simply to give myself the satisfaction of denouncing this weighty plea that I have written these pages. Long ago, I confess, I took occasion, when presenting to the French public an abridged history of the Oxford movement, to pay to Manning the signal homage that was in my heart. Led at first to study him closely by reason of the part he played in the great strike on the Thames docks, in 1889, I was not slow in passing from his social to his charitable and religious activity, and then to his whole personality. That exalted episcopal figure, so rigid and so modern, of such ascetic sanctity and of charity so broad; that devoted old priest, in this nineteenth century and in that Protestant country, in unrelaxing and uncompromising defence of what is most extreme in the most militant Catholicism, and, at the same time, with unbounded compassion and truly pastoral solicitude watching over all the sufferings of his people, why should I not give way to the powerful charm?

Newman acted forcibly on the mind—Newman, that subtle logician who stretched dialectics to the point of giving them an indescribable and disquieting tinge of casuistry; that bold idealist who was predestined to turn towards the eternal realities the looks of the inhabitants of a world in the material reality of which he

had never been able to believe; that Christian skeptic,
in fine, to whom the postulates of faith are the only
axioms of certitude, and who sees in the dogmas of
Revelation God's only answer to the doubts and
anguishes of reason.   Nothing would be more ungrateful than to want to reject a master at whose feet our
generation had so much to learn.   For my part, I
know what it has cost me to point out certain shadows
in the brightness of that pure glory, in order to refute
calumnies from which Manning has had to suffer too
much.   All of Mr. Purcell's evil spirit was needed to
rekindle these posthumous polemics.   Thank Heaven,
they cannot be perpetuated; those who have charitably
applauded and turned to account that myth of an
irreconcilable hostility between the two great restorers
of English Catholicism, will regret their brief joy.   In
the bosom of death, in the majestic unity of the eternal
Christianity, these little differences have disappeared,
and one can admire Manning without attacking Newman, or *vice versa*.   What attracts in such a subject is
not those retrospective controversies, it is in the first
place interest in that great spiritual risk.   In this restless age, when so many crafts wander compassless on
the waves, without a pilot and without a rudder, nothing consoles like the spectacle of a life that has dared
the high sea and the storms, that has approached many
shores, that has even had to part with its anchors after
having cast them there in desperation, and that at last
has entered port after incurring so many dangers.
There is, there ever will be, an almost irresistible attraction in the story of those lives that have described vast

parabolæ, that have known great heart-rendings and
have completed great sacrifices. If the history of a
Lamennais, beginning with faith—or at least with the
keen wish for faith, in a great struggle imposed on himself and on others—and ending in the most lamentable
of shipwrecks and in that species of the fierce isolation
of a Titan struck by lightning, who was indeed able to
renounce Christ but not to throw off his priestly robes
—if that tragic story has excited our contemporaries,
what an interest will not be offered by the striking contrast of the ascension of a man's soul, led step by step,
degree by degree, by the spirit of truth, of the elementary intuitions of faith, to the summits of revealed
religion and of the supernatural certitudes?

In the presence of these personages, so noble and so
melancholy, of a Lamennais, of a Jouffroy, of a
Scherer, on whose brows a ray of grace seemed to be
placed only to leave to them inconsolable regret for that
brightness forever lost, it is good to place the figure re-
splendent with light and joy of one of those whom God
led by the hand from the weak beginning of a still
rather imperfect conversion to the glorious consummation of the work of their salvation. If, in Manning's
case, this evolution was not accomplished without a
revolution; if he believed he ought to leave the Church
of his baptism, of his first communion and of his consecration, in order to go and ask of another Church
enfranchisement from the usurpations of the civil
power, the integral preservation of the deposit of faith,
the regularity of the Apostolic succession, the organization of discipline, the efficacy of the sacraments and

the reality of unity; if, born a Protestant, after twenty
years in the Anglican ministry he became a Catholic
and a priest, there is nothing in that which in advance
could have robbed him of respect or of sympathy. In
these matters, I feel certain, it suffices to merit or even
to obtain these feelings of good faith; and in kind it
could not be disputed, any more than Manning's dis-
interestedness or even his spirit of sacrifice. Without
entering for the moment into an examination of the
validity of the motives that directed him on this solemn
occasion, is it not just to show that the entire progress
of that internal evolution, from the first day on which
the young clergyman's attention was called to the
temporal role of the Holy Ghost and to the promises of
assistance made by our Lord Jesus Christ, until the
hour when he believed he had found its perfect realization in the authority of the Church and in the doctrinal
infallibility of the Sovereign Pontiff, was much less a
purely intellectual work than a labor of conscience? I
make bold to assert that any one who will without
prejudice read the documents, that is to say, the letters
and the fragments of a private diary, in the decisive
phase from 1847 to 1851, whatever judgment he passes
on the basis of things, and even indeed when he would
see in Manning's gradual approach towards Catholicism a capital and fatal error, will not be able to keep
from recognizing and proclaiming the sincerity of his
effort, the uprightness of his intentions, the growth of
his piety.

At first sight, this declaration—or this avowal—might
seem like a dilettante witticism or even a lesson in

skepticism. And yet who will pretend that God has promised to the individual soul the privilege of infallibility on all points as a reward for sanctity? When one writes the history of a man, prejudices, theories, doctrines themselves are of little importance; what there is question of taking hold of and reproducing is the life itself, acts, words, thoughts. I would have singularly falsified Manning's portrait if I had not painted, without taking the least concern in the world as to the consequences that might be derived from it in such or such a sense, the perfect sincerity of his *crisis:* the predominance in his thoughts of the great essential principles or rather of the constitutive facts of Christianity; his comparative indifference to a multitude of secondary problems in which certain minds want with all their might to see the necessary starting-point of every Catholicizing evolution; his ardent concern for the single question of salvation. There was one man, in any case, of whom one cannot say that, if he abjured Protestantism, it was from levity, for he struggled for six years against himself; or from a taste for the ceremonial and the pomps of worship, for his parish church when he left it was like St. Mary's at Oxford under Newman, of quite Evangelical simplicity and austerity; and Manning, once a Catholic, never gave to the external rites the disproportionate importance that the Ritualists give to them, in the bosom of Anglicanism. It is not from disdain for the Bible, for until the close of his life he made familiar, daily, continual use of it; nor from ambition, for, an archdeacon at thirty-two, at thirty-six he received the offer of a place that opened

to him the way to high dignities, and he was morally
sure of the Anglican episcopate, while in Catholicism,
then singularly despised and detested by the English
people, he was only a recruit and a novice. No, all
things agree in justifying the view that I thought 1
ought to take of this conversion, and in showing therein
an act of obedience and of faith in the first instance.
And it is not only for the understanding and apprecia-
tion of Manning's personality that this fact is of importance; it stands very high from the point of view of
the ideas of which the Archbishop of Westminster became the chief representative in the second part of his
career. If it is not a matter of indifference to recognize
that Catholicism and even Ultramontanism in Manning's case were the fruit of a spiritual development, it
is still less so to state that it was the same labor of conscience which produced the Cardinal's social conception.

From two opposite directions, two schools or two
parties strive to represent Catholicism or social Christianity as a sort of thoroughly lay or earthly doctrine,
devoid of every supernatural element, devoted only to
the solution of a problem, apparently difficult, by
means of human activity. Those who will not have
social Christianity because they hate the religion of
Christ, and those who will not have Christian socialism
because they hate the mere thought of an organic reform of society, meet certain men of more outspoken
zeal, but of ignorant good will, who rob this great movement of its meaning and its bearing. To bring religion
down to earth; to efface, or at least relegate to the back-

ground, everything Christian that is supernatural; to
treat dogma as out-of-date frippery that one completely
gets rid of by a sort of pious weakness for the past; to
make of human unity of action the alpha and omega of
morals without basing them on the fatherhood of God
revealed by the brotherhood of Christ; to transform the
Church into an immense workingmen's society, a
mutual aid syndicate or association; to want to work
the miracle of human love in the sphere of interests,
after having denied the miracle of Divine love on the
Cross; in a word, to pretend to renew mankind, to
establish the kingdom of justice and of charity upon
earth, without the aid of those great facts that contain
all of salvation,—the salvation of the species as well as
that of the individual,—such is the incoherent and un-
sound dream of minds that imagine they can strike two
blows with one stone, namely, dechristianize the
Church, and with this dechristianized Church regener-
ate the world. All would not formulate the object of
their secret wishes or of their unconscionable aspirations with this pitiless precision. There are souls still
half religious, but affected with the deadly contagion of
modern rationalism, for whom everything that dimin-
ishes the part of dogmatism and increases that of practical activity in the Church, brings it close to its vocation and makes it more in conformity with its Master's
design. It is often the noble error of ardent and generous hearts, touched to the quick by the sufferings and
injustice of our society, indignant at the indifference, I
had almost said the passive complicity, of the Church,
who aspire to seeing it fulfil its sacred mission, and who

lose sight of the fact that, without these dogmas for ego-
tistically meditating on which they reproach themselves,
she has neither mandate, nor strength, nor means of
action, nor motives. In our time, when it is so far
from easy to maintain unfailingly the testimony in
honor of the supernatural in Christianity and of Jesus
Christ, the miracle of miracles, nothing is as dangerous
as the coalition of a very practical rationalism with an
imprudent charity. And so one could not profess
enough gratitude towards the inflexible champions of
principles, who, while being the first to preach, and
that with incomparable ardor, the social crusade of the
Church, have taken care to connect it closely with the
profession of objective, dogmatic, orthodox Christianity. They have not only cleansed the Church of a
reproach; they have offered to the world the only
efficacious instrument of salvation. What particular
value, then, do they imagine that the quite natural,
quite human and earthly action of a great corporation
could have? Without a divine mandate, without the
assistance of its Master, without the Gospel to reawaken
conscience, without the sacraments to feed souls, what
would the Church be, what would it do, what even
could it hope for in social matters? Social Christianity
will be Christian in the full sense of the word, or it will
not be. This is what Manning set forth with incomparable force and clearness, not only in all that he said
and wrote on social Catholicism, in the closing years of
his life, but by his entire career. He believed that he
ought to become a Catholic, because he did not believe
he could otherwise remain a Christian; he was a Catho-

lic of authority and of centralization, by virtue of the
same need; in fine, he was the initiator of social Christianity or Catholicism because of his very fidelity to
doctrinal Catholicism. This whole evolution is maintained and is completed. It is one of the greatest
honors of Manning's memory that he was the first
representative—at least in his own country—of the
beneficent doctrine that the social encyclicals of Leo
XIII. have since then sanctioned and explained, and
the double object of which is to recall the Church to
the accomplishment of an essential part of its divine
vocation, and to offer to our sick society the remedy of
supernatural Christianity.

III.

There remains the question of principle that has
been put to me so insistently from several directions.
Certainly, I would by far have preferred not to have to
entertain the reader with things that emanate from the
conscience and in regard to which it seems to me that I
ought to impose a discreet silence upon myself. There
are subjects, however, that one should not treat in a
certain manner without taking at least the implicit
pledge to carry out his thought to the end, and to treat
with silence him who asks me to say more in the name
of what I have already said would be to fail in this.
Some have easily picked out from my articles a keen
sympathy not only for the man whose life I have
traced, but for some of the principles of which he was
the representative. They have put me in a position to
state clearly where I stand on the chapter of Catho-

licism.   If there was question only of the far from delicate curiosity that takes delight in flaunting scandal, or
even of that pitiless logic that wants at all hazards to
reach for you the extreme consequences of your own
assertions, no one, I am sure, would feel so ill disposed
towards me as to hold me to the impersonal expression
of my thought about them.   Some one tells me that I
have pained certain minds, hurt certain consciences; I
ought, then, to try and answer those solicitudes as
frankly as possible, and to explain myself as clearly as
I can on the condition of soul that caused these cares.

It should not cost me anything to acknowledge, in
the first place, the pleasure that I experienced, not
only in depicting the figure of a great Christian, but in
paying homage to a great Catholic.   Every question of
denominational allegiance set aside, it appeared to me
a priori that one of the best means of showing my respect for the spirit of the Reformation, that is to say,
apparently, for a mind that ought to be free from all
sectarian prejudice, ever ready to rise above differences
of form and of secondary disagreements so as to detect
the points of similarity and to hail the living unity of
the invisible Church, was to trace freely, but lovingly,
the portrait of a man like Manning.   This way of prac-
tically putting to a test the breadth of certain doctrin-
aires of religious liberalism has not been too successful
with me.   In general, people have not forgiven the
Cardinal, the Ultramontane, the pervert from Protestantism because he was a friend of the poor, an ascetic,
an imitator of Christ.   They have not even appeared
to understand the peculiar role of the historian and

that, when one wishes to make a man live again, it is necessary to penetrate into his soul, to catch there his most secret movements, to share his feelings, to make his affections one's own, to see through his eyes, to speak with his mouth, in a word, to assume his personality. What a pleasant method in history, and especially in biographical history, is that which shuts you up as it were behind a triple padlock in your I, which builds a Chinese wall or an ice rampart between your hero and you, and which forbids you in advance to use that marvelous key, sympathy! No doubt, there exists a condition preliminary to the use of this means, and it is precisely because there is a previous harmony between him whom you have chosen and yourself; it is because you have not to contract yourself in order to get into his skin; it is, in a word, because he is indeed a hero to you.

I no longer know which of my critics it was who poked pleasant fun at the term, *a hero of charity*, which I had applied to Manning. He notes that the Cardinal died in his bed, an octogenarian—and while bantering. For my part, I was unaware until then that it was absolutely necessary to die young and by a violent death in order to merit this name, and I had thought that some one had said: heroic charity, that some one had said: heroic probity, heroic justice, to indicate a certain supernatural degree of virtue to which a man cannot rise without the aid of grace. In any case, there is my confession made, and if professing a profound admiration for the man whose life one writes is ruling oneself out of court and having his cause rejected for manifest partiality, I have merited this verdict. That is not all. Called upon to be concerned in the first instance with Manning's evolution such as it was produced in fact, to follow out its bent, to see things at the same angle as he, I thought I ought to accept the same data of the problem, such as it was laid down before him. I generalized as little as possible. The great trial of Protestantism and of Catholicism, for example, was pleaded for him on the rather narrow and artificial ground of Anglicanism. He had to choose not between religion and authority and religion and liberty, but between the religion of authentic, legitimate and real authority and the religion of factitious and illusory authority. He himself was perfectly conscious of this circumstance, which up to a certain point modified the value of his conclusions. At the moment of his taking the decisive step and of performing the irrevocable act which from his being an Anglican made him a Catholic, he so distinctly felt that it was not Protestantism in itself of which he experienced the insufficiency, that he admitted the possibility of going to the mystic idealism of the invisible Church, that is to say, to the true conception of the Reformation, quite as much as to the objective realism of Rome. He excluded only one part, return to the pseudo-Catholicism, linked with pseudo-Protestantism, of the Anglican Church.

That is a fact the memory of which ought not to be lost sight of while reading these pages. In Manning's thought, under a naturally rather confused and imperfect form, in the thought of him who is writing these lines, in a much more clearly defined form—the greater part of the difficulties, objections, criticisms, reproaches and grievances that at last led the Archdeacon of Chichester to Rome, were addressed not to that very slightly metaphysical entity, Protestantism in itself, but to that quite real and quite special institution, the Church of England.

It would be unjust, then, merely to detach from their context and without any more ado apply to Protestantism in itself arguments or imputations that pertain to that very particular form of religion, Anglicanism. It is even quite pointed to see certain extreme champions of Protestantism, in their ignorant zeal, take under their protection an ecclesiastical establishment which absolutely refuses to stand on their principles, which repudiates all solidarity with them, and which, as is proved by a very beautiful passage in the first Pastoral Letter of Manning as Archbishop of Westminster, on the attitude of the Church towards dissidents, would, in all probability, in the name of the Anglo-Catholic pretensions, show itself much more aggressive and unjust than is Catholicism towards Protestant Nonconformism. This means—and I would have been lacking in truth if I had not said it—that I would be very blind indeed to higher truth if I did not add immediately that it would have been much more difficult for me as an historian to identify myself with my hero or to reproduce with their full force arguments which, while bearing on Anglicanism, do not leave Protestantism to some extent untouched, if I had not felt a real sympathy for the very groundwork of Manning's ideas.

I do not know, in truth, whether I will succeed, I

4

do not say in having others share with me, but in
making them understand, the state of mind that dictated to me and that in my own estimation justifies my
attitude on these questions: authorized and obliged, as
I think I am, to write all that I have written—without
eliminating a word from it—and at the same time to do
only what I have done, without going a step farther.
To conceive that, if there be a Church—in the Catholic
sense of the word—there is only one, and it is that one
whose centre is at Rome; to profess that, if Christianity
is not merely the religion of individualism pure and
simple, if, outside the mystic communion of the soul
with its Saviour there is the solidarity and the common
life of the members of Christ's body, the Christian organism implies the decisive role of tradition and authority; to believe that, if the promised succor, the
assistance of the Holy Ghost, does not bear merely on
the personal assurance of salvation, the providential
preservation of the deposit of faith requires a whole
objective mechanism; to see in the sacraments, if they
are not merely the mnemotechnic signs of the great
facts of Redemption, powerful realities, incomparable
means of grace and of life; to understand that, since
reason is not the court of last resort for matters of faith,
it ought to disavow the principle of free examination
and to acknowledge the sovereignty of another judge:
there is a whole collection of sentiments that will perhaps perforce scandalize Protestants, without fully sat-
isfying Catholics. That is not all; at the same time as
my mind was being opened to the somewhat hypotheti-
cal intuition of the living unity of the Catholic system,

experience revealed to me the practical consequences of
certain Protestant premises. It is not without some
emotion, let me be allowed to say here, that I approach
this ground. Two years ago, speaking on an analogous
subject, before an entirely Protestant audience, in an
entirely Protestant city that I had chosen on purpose, I
declared that, rather than utter certain words and expose myself to certain interpretations in surroundings
whose atmosphere would be radically different and
saturated with all other elements, I would prefer to put
my hand on my mouth and remain silent. If to-day I
break that silence, it is because I am compelled to do
so, and imagine that I cannot better touch on these
delicate questions than by tracing in all honesty the
steps taken by my thought. Protestantism in its entirety, and particularly in French-speaking countries,
has for some time felt itself on the eve of a dread crisis.
Theological science is in the act of communicating not
only to the clergy, but to the body of the faithful also,
the chief results of its great labors in criticism and in
speculation.

To-day the watchword is: No more private study!
no more dualism, more or less conscious and acknowledged, between what is elaborated in the study and
what is preached in the pulpit. Frankness, frankness,
and again frankness! Is it necessary for me to say
how far this movement seems to me lawful or rather
imperative? Assuredly it would be a calumny on our
fathers—the men of those generations that gathered and
handed down to us the inheritance of faith and zeal of
the *Reawakening*—to attribute to them, in any degree

whatever, the intention of keeping the laity apart—or sheltered—from the results of theological culture. There was neither plot, nor conspiracy, nor even fixed purpose. This sort of dualism was produced because in fact most of the leaders themselves were still tied up in the bonds of the older conceptions and would have been very much embarrassed in communicating to their flocks hypotheses, moreover, still far from settled and by no means under control, and systems still in the condition of conjectures. Nevertheless, it is now a long time since one of the ideas on which the Re-awakening generation thought they should have fixed the edifice of their faith,—the idea of theopneustics or the plenary inspiration of Sacred Scripture,—found themselves singularly shaken. One would not at the present time, I think, meet many declared orthodox persons who would not sign with both hands, at least as regards the fundamental principles, Edmond Scherer's famous pamphlet, so furiously denounced in 1848. But that was only a beginning. It is not sufficient to destroy the unaffected confidence that sees in each book, in each page, in each line, in each word of the Bible a direct and authentic revelation, a word imme-diately from God. It is necessary to point out to the souls of the simple-minded, astonished and frightened at this great void, what will take the place of the authority of the Bible. And everywhere, on all points at the same time, this two-fold work is being carried on: on the one hand, completing the overthrow of the erroneous conceptions of the past; on the other, substi-tuting for them notions more in conformity with the present criteria of theological truth, and capable at the same time of offering, as heretofore, a support to religious, individual and collective life. One would not be much astonished at these two parts of the work not advancing on the same path.

Demolitions always take place more rapidly than rebuildings. It is easier to ruin the theopneustic hypothesis, to destroy the unity, authenticity and antiquity of the Pentateuch, to refer necessarily the whole history of Israel to the royal period as the starting point and to the pretended post-exile texts as dated documents, than to reconstruct an acceptable and especially likely theory of the authority of the Bible and of the character of the Old Testament.

Now, it must be remembered that historically Protestantism has lived on a twofold principle; first, that which is called *formal*, the authority of the Sacred Scriptures; second, material, justification by faith. These two principles are confined within a narrow mutual dependence. The former affirms that Jesus Christ is the only source of the knowledge of salvation, that every human soul directly and personally receives the light necessary to distinguish God's message in the documents of the history of Redemption; the second, that Jesus Christ alone is the source of salvation, that direct and immediate contact with the Saviour, even outside of every external means of grace, suffices for every human soul in order to receive the plenitude of Redemption. Is it not too evident that the former of these fundamental axioms of the Reformation,—Jesus Christ, the only and sufficient source of the knowledge of salvation through Sacred Scripture, without tradition and without interpreter,—is, if not strictly imperiled, at least surrounded with strange difficulties, owing to the progress of criticism? Of old it seemed quite simple to the most ignorant, to the most modest of the faithful, to lend an ear to that voice of God which alone, in the written form, he ought to obey as he would his conscience. He took up his Bible, he turned over its leaves, and each word shone in his eyes like a divine word. Now, when he opens the Sacred Book, he has to begin with asking himself: Is this part indeed authentic? Is this word so? Is it a discourse by Jesus Christ or a marginal note by St. John that I am reading? Is it the original narrative of an eye-witness, or is it not rather the tendency deposit of the historical transactions and compromises of Judæo-Christian diplomacy, that I am consulting? Oh! I know the answer that one makes: the inner meaning, the experience of the Christian suffices for him to discern the sound of the Master's voice. But, in fine, this very principle has its limits, under penalty of falling into absolute subjectivism, into the only sovereignty of the *testimonium spiritus*. There must be something objective; it must be that faith has something to take hold of; it must be that conscience, in order to find the wherewith to be satisfied, meet something that exceeds it in every meaning and of which it cannot set itself up as an infallible judge. The Reformers, I think, would have far from enjoyed, in their robust common sense and their need of the positive, those subtle theories by which, under the pretext of driving to its last extremity the second of their formulas, namely, Jesus Christ the only source of salvation, and, consequently, of reducing to a minimum the importance of the accessory elements and, if one dare say so, of the external element of that great redeeming fact, one sets a low price on that authority of the Scriptures to which on their part they attach no less value and in which they see the means by which Christ had wished to assure the objective knowledge of His work. Moreover, one does not stop such a work of decomposition where one would like: when the authority of the Scriptures is directly attacked one has not long to wait to see the very person of the Saviour also suffer. Those who pretend, with the best faith in the world, I am convinced, to crack the nut in order the better to taste the fruit that it conceals, to break the vase in order the better to inhale the perfume that it contains, must sooner or later acknowledge that they have followed a dangerous chimera.

The famous theological renovation bears on all points at the same time. It extends over every domain. It is dogmatics, for example, by which it is demonstrated to us that there are no dogmas in the Gospel; that dogma is purely and simply the subjective and intellectual expression of a given condition of soul; that evolution, in the strict sense, Darwinian, from the word, presides over the formation of dogmas; that religion, in its final analysis, is reduced, according to Matthew Arnold's witty and profound expression, to *morality touched by emotion*. It is a theory of knowledge that people pretend to impose on us by reason of a previous condition of all speculation in religious matters and which fixes the relativity of every judgment, the radical impossibility of every assertion bearing on essence or of every objective concept.   It is a theology which in the first instance declares that God, as far as it is concerned, is, and could be, only the sum total of ideas in relation to the Divinity that may be found in the sum total of minds; that the I, moreover, is itself also but a conscious sequence of localized sensations implicitly asserting their mutual dependence; that, in fine, the veritable restoration of Christianity, that is, of the power of life and salvation in mankind that we cannot do without, implies the previous acceptance of Kant's criticism going beyond Kant, or rather of Hume's skepticism and the formal repudiation of realism in all domains.   It is Ritschl who is the prophet of this new dispensation, as Schleiermacher was of an anterior phase, and, after Hegel, it is Kant and Hume, with Darwin riding behind, who must serve as masters to this finally authentic interpreting of Christian revelation.   I certainly do not pretend that these doctrines already have the right of citizenship in every pulpit of Protestantism; but are they not often the matter of the teaching given to the future members of the clergy? Are they not floating in the air?   Do we not hear, as a characteristic symptom, of connecting paths, paved with good intentions, showing that, after all, there is a great deal of truth and common sense in these ideas; that dogma has always made the religious atmosphere thicker and heavier; that the living and holy person of the Saviour will be so much the more clearly evident and in close and direct communion with us as the

shadow of dogmatism will have ceased to weigh upon
it? Do not people speak of necessary reconciliations
with the representatives of the so-called liberal theology
which the preceding generation thought it had to combat energetically and to eliminate as much as possible
from the bosom of the Church? Is not the atmosphere
quite filled with the sound of these Lamourette kisses
that must, we are assured, put an end to the scandal of
the sons of the Huguenots, but by substituting for it
another more serious scandal, that of the cordial understanding in one and the same Church between Christians and philosophers, between believers and free-
thinkers?

In reality, it is towards anti-dogmatism that people
are tending, towards a religion in which dogma will
play a part, if not negative, at least very subordinate,
and in which the same stroke will complete the evap-
orating of whatever might remain of the idea of a
Church, of that of the means of grace and of the sacraments. I certainly do not pretend in a melancholy
way to describe a universal condition of affairs, I but
note tendencies. Thank God, everybody knows that,
even in the most falsified frameworks, in the most imperfect forms, enough religious life remains to feed
powerful currents. Who could be sufficiently blinded
by party or sectarian spirit not to point out with joy
that, in the Churches of the Reformation as well as in
the Catholic Church, there are lives of the saints,
triumphal deaths, splendid examples of the omnipo-
tence of grace, and that the only indisputable apostolic
succession—that which assures to Christ and to man-

kind an uninterrupted line of zealous servants full of
faith—does not allow of any service outside of the very
narrow limits of an historic communion?   It would be
right to ask an accounting for such arrogant severity
from any one who would undertake to issue wholesale
condemnations against men whose shoestrings they
would most frequently not be worthy to loose.

Such, I dare believe, is not the feeling that I obey
on this occasion.   Does any one really imagine that
filial piety is so easily wiped out, and that it is so easy
to fail in respect to the memory of those to whom we
owe all that we can have, I do not say merely of religion, but of conscience and of honor?   Is it so presumptuous, then, while feeling the sincerest gratitude,
the most tender veneration for the memories that are
dear to you, to acknowledge to oneself that one could
not live on the faith that sufficed to a soul nearer to
God and less subject to the powers of evil?   I am astonished, in truth, that people do not deign to see what
true humility there can be in the uneasiness of a conscience that cannot be satisfied as to its own salvation
with a doctrine in which it does not doubt that those
whom it most loves and respects have found the most
ample and most solid satisfaction of all their needs.   A
perfectly upright and pure soul, one of those natures
in which, as was said with happy boldness by the
great Christian philosopher, Charles Sécretan, original
sin is reduced to its congruous share, is for that very
reason even in a measure enfranchised from the conditions that impose a whole order of pressing needs on an
average and mediocre nature.   It can uncover elements

of life and take possession of them and prosper in an atmosphere in which a less happily gifted soul will suffocate and blanch. There are consciences which, in order to enter into direct relation with their Saviour, have only to get a glimpse at His divine figure in a flash. Their rapid and sure flight has no need of carefully cleared paths, of ladders or of steps held up with great difficulty, which the heavier, slower and more human step of less privileged beings could not do without. A sort of preëstablished harmony between the Master and some disciples allows the latter to hear and to make sure of recognizing His voice, without their having to be on their guard for the external signs and the infallible marks which the great bulk of the flock could not disregard without danger. Fortunate navigators have been seen to reach port in a little bark, without an official pilot, without a rudder, almost without a compass, whilst the bulk of the passengers could not without the most dangerous presumption take the liberty of going up on the disciplined ship's deck, but had to watch her from their berths, and to obey the orders issued by the lawful authorities so as not to embarrass them in their work.

No one, I think, will pretend that to humbly acknowledge oneself condemned to the royal highways is to set oneself up as a judge of those to whom God allows the by-ways. If, to a few select souls, grace is to some extent independent of dogma, it does not follow either that, as far as everybody is concerned, dogma can be directly attacked with impunity without grace having to suffer from it, or that one is disputing grace

to the former when claiming for oneself the solid
support of dogma. God works in favor of some the
miracle of a salvation in a certain sense individual,
which passes through extraordinary channels. If it
has been justly and strongly said that there are atheists
who force belief in God and who have too many virtues
not to be Christians in fact, how much the more should
we not say that there are men whom the imperfections
of their Church and of their theology could not rob of
the possession of the one thing necessary? To count
for oneself on this exceptional regime would be to
tempt God; to seek for oneself in all sincerity the
ordinary conditions of grace, is not to pass any judgment on these privileged persons. It is above all to
proclaim one's own weakness; it is to confess that one
is more accessible to the deleterious influences of an
unhealthy atmosphere; it is to acknowledge that, without the supports and succors of tradition and authority,
one feels his faith give way, that dogma could not be
clouded in your eyes without grace being affected, that
the results of modern theology or of the unrestricted
exercise of the faculty of criticism and of free examination, if they do not find a corrective and a necessary
counterpoise, undermine in your soul even the very
foundations of the work of Redemption. I can see
most clearly how one points out, denounces, mocks,
if one wishes, the strange mental debility, namely, the
weakness of will of those who confess this need of authority: I absolutely deny that one has the right to
cast moral opprobrium on this attitude and from on
high to condemn in it some indescribable want of re-

spect in those who until the end have practised the individualistic religion, and from whose inheritance one has received an entirely Protestant name. This argument comes with particularly bad grace from the mouth of those who have made of free examination a sort of intellectualist dogma, who admit of no exemption from the sovereign jurisdiction of criticism, and who, apparently, do not dispute the exercise by the Reformers of the right of revising tradition and of revoking to some extent the conclusions of those very persons from whom they had received the deposit of faith. If the Reformation was able legitimately to go back through the course of ages and to rub out the twelve or thirteen centuries of Catholic evolution, because of the consequences, fatal in their estimation, of the principle of authority, one could not invoke any exception against those who are pre-concerned by the consequences of the principle of individualism and who seek to go back up the current and again to lay hold of the living unity of Christendom.

Who, then, among those who still adhere to the religion of the supernatural, of the Incarnation of the Son of God and of the Redemption by the Cross, does not feel alarmed at the more or less insidious progress of the tendency that is shaking the authority of the Sacred Scriptures, and that is reducing to the rank of a mere mortal, no matter how incomparable He might have been, the Christ of the Expiation and of the Justification? Who has not sometimes asked himself with anguish whether, after all, it was not the legitimate use of the processes set in honor by the Reformation that

ended in striking to the very heart the fundamental
dogmas or rather facts of the religion that saves? Are
there not moments when the most pronounced optimist,
the person most convinced that the schism of the sixteenth century was willed by God and restored truths
forgotten or effaced by Catholicism, questions himself
regarding the solidity of a Church which rests on justification by faith and on the inspiration and authority
of the Scriptures, and who sees these two foundations
directly attacked with the very weapons which it
thought it made use of in their defence? It is a painful situation in which it seems at certain moments that
it is necessary to choose between the very principles
and the objects of the Reformation—between the
method which it inaugurated as the only proper one in
matters of faith and the realization of the ideal of
Christian life which it had proposed to itself.

It is seen that there is not question in that, as critics
devoid of good faith have wanted to make believe, of I
know not what romantic reaction, of a St. Martin's
Summer of neo-Catholicism after the manner of Cha-
teaubriand, of a need of æsthetic emotions. Whether
wrongly or rightly, it is the very essence of Christianity
that one believes to be in question, and one asks oneself from many points of view whether the supernatural
in Christianity is not far safer in a Church which professes to be in possession of the plenitude of the means
of grace, in a religious society over which the ages have
passed, and which claims or which offers in the Apostolic succession, in the primacy of Peter's see, in its
whole hierarchical organization, in all the objective

realities of its worship, the threefold guarantee of unity, authority and perpetuity. After all, history has its teachings. When one sees the Anglo-Catholic movement ending, not only in the abjuration of its chief initiators, but in the transformation of Anglicanism; when one witnesses the efforts of that great Church separated for three centuries from the centre of Roman unity in order to regain possession, without, however, paying its price, of the advantages of the Catholic system; when one sees it reclaim the Apostolic succession for its bishops, the validity of the ordination of its ministers, restore the Eucharistic service and even the sacrifice of the Mass, practise confession and the sacrament of penance, seeking to set up orders again, in brief, borrowing from the Papal Church all that can make its strength, but nothing of what would constitute an act of submission, one cannot help feeling a certain uneasiness. Those, then, are the revenges of Catholicism—revenges, no doubt, against an ecclesiastical establishment which has ever borne in its constitution the germ of all contradictions, and which smacks of the opposing interests, doctrines and wills of the politicians who were its founders—and likewise in the heart of the classic country of individualist Protestantism; on the morrow of the great Evangelical reawakening; in the presence of the upspringing of those non-conformist Churches that are entirely penetrated with the spirit of the Reformation. And that is not all. Our generation sees itself confronted, with an urgency from day to day more imperious, by a whole order of questions in which the very principle of indi-

vidualism seems in advance to have been disabled from
fighting.

In this great social evolution of which all have a
presentiment, certain symptoms of which are already
making themselves felt, which must be brought about
at any price if our social organisms want to spare themselves a revolution and if justice be truly the reason for
their existence, is it indeed the Christianity of the
Reformation that will be able to play the part of leaven
and of spiritual ferment? Will it bring forth at the
right time, not only Ch. Sécretans, thinkers who will
state the problem and who will study it under all its
aspects, but Mannings and Gibbonses, those pillars of
the Church's power, whenever there is poverty to be
assuaged and charity to be organized? I well know
that Protestantism has had its Shaftesbury; but will
the miracle of a truly divine big-heartedness combined
with unequaled narrowness of thought, that alliance or
that alloy of heroic charity with a sort of morbid
shrinking of the mind, be found again? and, if it were
found again, would it suffice for our time? In fine, is
there not in souls at this time, side by side with the
passion for enjoyments and dilettantism, a need of renunciation, asceticism, discipline, obedience, holy and
secluded life, activity and contemplation, regulated and
cloistered, as it is ever felt in the epochs of decadence
and of dissolution or of moral and social decomposition,
when they have still in them a germ of resurrection and
of life,—as in the fourth and fifth centuries of our era?
—needs that are not perhaps incompatible with the
very spirit of the Reformation, but which, however, can

at present hardly find organized and regular satisfaction outside of Catholicism?

Monachism has its place in the Catholic system; and I do not know whether the Protestant system, even by modifying it on essential points, would find a place for it. And as for those mystical needs of a closer union, of a more complete penetration, of a possession at the same time more immediate and more objective, are not the sacraments such as the Catholic Church honors and administers them better calculated to quench a thirst than it could be satisfied by the commemorations to which Protestantism—at least outside of Luther's Church—has too often reduced the most solemn acts of the religious life?

Without belittling the austere grandeur that is sometimes assumed by the Reformed worship, when it does not remotely ape the externals of Catholic ceremonies, and when the imagination knows how to trace the historical causes of that simplicity and of that bareness, I may be allowed to say that one feels on every side in Protestantism the need of profound renovation. A form of worship presenting the daily repetition of the great drama of the Expiation, with the incessantly renewed symbols of the single Sacrifice of the Cross, with the majestic accents of a liturgy whose roots plunge into the heart of a primitive Christendom, with a constant attestation of the Communion of Saints and of the indefectible union of the Church of Christ, seems better adapted to attract and to hold souls weary of the subtleties of analysis, of the dryness of reason and of the sophistry of doubt. I do not consider myself the only

5

one feeling all that, and feeling it strongly; and yet it is certain that, while sometimes experiencing a sort of intellectual and moral haunting, while sometimes asking whether one is not resisting his conscience, no one hitherto has been able either to throw off a painful uncertainty or especially to decide on one of those irrevocable steps that are lawful only when they are forced.

Undoubtedly, it is good to say to oneself that at a certain height the most divergent lines meet; that there is a level at which a St. Augustine, a St. Vincent de Paul, a Pascal and a Manning are inundated with the same rays of light and glory and make the same triumphant chants resound as do a Luther, a Coligny, a Franke, a Vinet and a Shaftesbury. It is sweet to recall with what sovereign breadth certain great Christians have been pleased to forget their secondary disagreements and to celebrate their accord on the fundamental points of faith, like that venerable priest of the diocese of Paris who felt himself pressed to associate in his sacerdotal jubilee the prayers of his friend, a Protestant pastor. All that is beneficent; but one must not indulge in fictions too agreeable nor take refuge in a sort of cloudy idealism. Have we not just witnessed the failure of one of those premature attempts, in which the desire for conciliation gains the upper hand over the search for conditions of agreement; in which some one says: Peace, peace, where there is no peace, and which necessarily end, in spite of the best intentions, in the most complete broils? On February 14, 1895, Lord Halifax said to the members of the English Church Union at Bristol that union with Rome is desirable, is possible. He expressed a wish to see the Church of Rome make to the Anglican Church overtures calculated to *bring on corporate reunion*. Leo XIII.'s letter "Ad Anglos" was in a certain sense the Sovereign Pontiff's answer to this request, and some have been able to say that they heard in it the voice of a father. Ardent souls conceived the hope of a prompt return of the Anglican Church to unity with Rome. Great illusions were entertained, chimeras were fostered even, until the Encyclical "Satis Cognitum" came to formulate the conditions necessary for any reconciliation, and to reiterate with the authority of the successor of St. Peter the lesson that Manning had already given in his Pastoral of 1866 to the compromise intermediators. Between Catholicism, even when it is represented by a Leo XIII., and Protestantism, even when it has reduced to a minimum its profession of the principles of the Reformation and strives, like the Anglicanism of Lord Halifax, to follow a *via media* equally distant from Rome and from Geneva, any dealing is hardly possible; it seems that it is necessary to submit or to fight. That is an acknowledgment that one is sometimes compelled to make to oneself, after having most sincerely dreamt of factitious agreements or of alliances against nature—vain illusions.

The Churches of the Reformation and the Catholic Church no doubt have in common the eternal Christianity, that which makes the deposit of revelation and of faith—but under what different, or rather contrary, forms is this common basis dissimulated! Truly, there is no halfway halting between the temple and the

cathedral.   It is deliberate, conscious choice between
the two that one ought to know how to look in the face.
If ever this painful alternative be imposed upon one of
us, may God keep him from ever forgetting what he
owes to the religion of the fathers!   It is to them, it is
often to a father, in the singular, that a son owes the
little Christianity that makes him live.   Therein for
some consists the inner drama that is brutally turned
to advantage by controversialists who see in all that
only a matter for controversy.   Can it not sometimes
happen that it is for being faithful to the spirit, to the
lessons, to the principles of those to whom one owes
the knowledge of salvation, that one feels tempted to
show oneself unfaithful to his teaching?

The guilt would consist in acting with levity; in paying attention to other words than those of conscience;
in rejecting the memory of those great effects of grace
that have stood out prominently in the communion in
which one was born; in repudiating the memory of
those generous, chivalrous, honest and pure lives,
entirely devoted to the service of God and of men, of
those still more glorious dead in whom the power of
divine life has been manifested with incomparable
strength.   When one's heart is in the right place, one
scarcely risks giving all his weight to these considerations; but it would be none the less culpable to plug
one's ears with sentimental reminiscences and not to
listen to the imperious appeal of conscience, if ever it
says to you: The work of demolition is going on; to
others perhaps it brings no danger, but not to you; the
supernatural in Christianity, the dogmas of the Gospel

vanish under the scalpel of the higher criticism; the object of faith, all objective religion, is reduced to the nebulous state; theology gives us a Bible whose disjointed pieces require to be printed in different colors, and which scholars only, after close research, will still be able to read with discernment; it presents to us an impalpable, intangible Christ, a sort of twilight phantom, fallen at the same time from His divinity and from His humanity, without historical reality in the past, without celestial reality in the present, without supernatural reality in the sacraments. The cup that is offered to us is full of a deadly beverage—let us reject this poison! Like the woman in the Gospel, rather than let Christ escape, perhaps it will be necessary for our generation to take hold of the hem of His garment; perhaps it will be even necessary for it to follow in the footsteps of His disciples, even were it only to be touched by that shadow of Peter healing the sick of Jerusalem.

PART SECOND.

MANNING AS A PROTESTANT.

A FEW months apart, four years ago,* there died in England two old men, loaded with days and with works, two cardinals of the holy Roman Church, two of the men who, in this faithless age, and in a country separated from the centre of unity since the Reformation, contributed most to restoring Catholicism to a place of honor and giving back to it the prestige and authority of one of the greatest spiritual forces of our time. One of these two great deceased passed away from the exhaustion of extreme old age in a monastic house in a suburb of Birmingham, and the modest coffin of that Oratorian—whom the purple, coming to him late in life, had not drawn out of his studious retreat—received the homage of the pick of intellectual England, proud to salute in John Henry Newman one of the masters of that bold controversialism, of that subtle psychology and of that fearless logic the imperishable model of which, on certain points, was supplied by Pascal, and which subjects reason to an apparent skepticism only to cast it at the foot of the Cross. The other, not so old, but worn out by the fatigues of

* This was written in the spring of 1896.

devouring activity and by the practices of strict asceticism, heaved his last sigh in that plain house in Westminster where he had wished to fix his archiepiscopal residence. He expired almost at the same hour as the young Duke of Clarence; and one might have believed that, in a profoundly loyalist and monarchical, and moreover Protestant, nation, both in name and in traditions, the regrets caused by the premature end of the heir presumptive to the crown would have scarcely left room for mourning this octogenarian, this pervert from Anglicanism, this head of English Catholicism. None the less on that account did his funeral assume the imposing, sublime, unique character of a great popular demonstration. It was a whole people—the people of work, of poverty and of suffering—that arose to mourn a hero of charity.

That, assuredly, was a sight which scarcely any one had expected in the England of the last decade of the nineteenth century. No one, so much as the former of these princes of a Church whose communion England deserted three and a half centuries ago, had buffeted proud reason; had heaped scorn on practical materialism; had disdained or rather ignored those improvements so much boasted of, those famous mechanical inventions, those pretended conquests of science, blind admiration for which constitutes almost entirely the religion of many of our contemporaries. No one had given as much scandal as Cardinal Manning to that Anglicanism of which he had formerly been the pillar and the hope, to that vulgar Liberalism which sees no enemy but in the Church, and no liberty but in the oppression of consciences, to that stiff and formal clericalism from which he had freed himself by the very power of his religious and ecclesiastical convictions, to that economical orthodoxy, in fine, whose commonplaces are so agreeable to the egoism of certain classes, and in violating all of whose laws and disputing all of whose principles he had often seemed to take pleasure. And that is not all. Both of those renovators of Catholicism had gone out from Protestantism after having rent it asunder. The first half of their lives, in the one case as in the other, had been devoted to the service of the Anglican Church, in the ranks of its clergy. Both of them, though in different degrees, had been leaders of a party; they had fought for the Church of their fathers, against Rome and its pretentions. They had stopped souls on the incline of desertion and of submission to the authority of the Vicar of Jesus Christ. It was one of them who had inaugurated and for twelve years directed that great Anglo-Catholic movement, the command of which the second picked up and held for some time after it had fallen from the faithless hands of the commander-in-chief, when the latter passed over to the enemy in 1845. It was they who had given the impetus to that great current whose wave at last cast them in spite of themselves on the opposite shore, but not until after they had fertilized the hitherto rather sterile and unyielding soil of Anglicanism, and had made a whole harvest of piety, spiritual life and works of charity germinate there.

We see how, by one of those bounds that defy calculation and confound reason, England, after all Protestant, Anglican and especially anti-Papal, has celebrated and honored in these two men two of the greatest enemies of those compromises that are dear to her in religion as well as in politics, two revolutionists resolved on overthrowing, in the name of the absolute, that regime of the ecclesiastical mean to which she is so strongly attached. The history of these two lives can alone explain this apparent paradox. Truly, these biographies, if we add to them that of Pusey and of some other personages of secondary rank, properly constitute the entire history of Anglo-Catholicism.

I do not pretend to write it here. I can do nothing now but draw a hasty sketch of a subject which, like Jansenism in the seventeenth century, would require, in order to be treated as it deserves, conscientious erudition, delicate psychology, the incomparable method of Sainte-Beuve in his "Port-Royal." This great memory, this perilous analogy, impresses itself upon any one who has penetrated even but a little way into the study of that great religious movement, which traverses the history of contemporary England as the Jansenist movement traverses the history of France under Louis XIII. and Louis XIV. Yes, this agitation, inaugurated by a few young members of the university and parish clergy, without any other headquarters than the common hall of the Fellows or tutors of Oriel College, without any other leader than an obscure young priest whose genius had not yet been revealed to himself, and who had scarcely broken loose from the tightened bonds of the Protestantism called Evangelical, produced in the religion and society of England, I

make bold to say, a revolution that is no less extensive
and no less profound than that brought about at the
same time in the body politic by the great Parliamentary reform.   It is radically impossible, without taking
a somewhat accurate view of Anglo-Catholicism, to
form a correct idea of modern England—I mean of
political, social and literary England quite as much as
of religious, ecclesiastical and moral England.   If one
has every reason to say: There is an England preceding and an England following the Reform Act of 1832,
one can and one ought to say: There is an England
preceding and an England following the "Tracts for
the Times."   Keble's famous sessional sermon, the
condemnation of Tract No. 90, the censuring of Ward,
Newman's conversion and that of Manning, are dates
not only in the history of the Oxford movement, but in
that of England in the nineteenth century.

It is this which explains why the English public
cannot grow weary of hearing reference made to that
drama of the religious conscience.   Since the day, now
already far distant, when Newman, in order to repel
Kingsley's gross insinuations, wrote the "Apologia
pro Vita Sua," a masterpiece of spiritual autobiography,
of psychological analysis, of intellectual subtlety and
of moral candor, worthy to appear alongside of St.
Augustine's "Confessions," how many publications of
all sorts—memoirs, correspondence, lives, historical
essays, mere articles—have accumulated on that inexhaustible theme?   There is still wanting, no doubt, the
master work that will collect all these scattered elements, that will group all these materials and that will

raise the definitive edifice, in proper proportions and on solid foundations. The interesting, but incomplete and hasty, abridgment written by Dean Church, of St. Paul's, cannot pass for having filled this gap. Perhaps it never will be filled. Perhaps, if it be not too presumptuous to acknowledge such an ambition here, it will be from whence it might be least expected—from outside, by a foreign hand—that the wished-for work will come. In the meantime this summary sketch and the monumental biographies of Newman, Pusey, and now of. Manning, already enable us to take in vast horizon expanses at a glance. The *dii minores*, the Kebles, the Wards, the Richard Hurrell Froudes, the Robert and Henry Wilberforces, the Isaac Williamses, the Charles Marriotts, those *twelve good men* of whom Dean Burgon has left us a portrait gallery, have been exposed in full daylight. As for memoirs, they abound: Palmer's recollections, J. B. Mozley's letters, Thomas Mozley's babbling and tattling reminiscences, that far from edifying "Ana" of a religious cenacle, that parading behind the scenes of a Church party by an ecclesiastic who is worldly and passably skeptic, in spite, or rather because, of his cloth.

The confessions of the shipwrecked of Anglo-Catholicism must be put in a separate class. Unfortunates were they who felt Newman's influence just enough to repudiate the agreeable compromises and the conveniences of the official and current religion, not enough to spring forward and plant themselves solidly on the rock of dogmatism, of the faith of authority; who became inoculated with the mystic fever only to reawaken shivering and prostrated after the attack, and whom a passing wave of Catholicism let fall back into discouraged skepticism or militant agnosticism. Such was Francis Newman, John Henry's younger brother, a restless, wandering spirit, at first a missionary in Persia, then a Deist in England; in every respect the opposite of his glorious elder brother, to whom, however, he was united by one of those paradoxical resemblances arising from the similarity of special traits and from the contrast of the whole. He is the author of "Phases of Faith" and of that curious and sorry pamphlet which he thought he had to lay on his brother's scarcely closed tomb. Such also was James Anthony Froude, the historian, the younger brother of Richard Hurrell, who grew up at Newman's knees, for a long time the most fervent of disciples and the most docile of novices, whom the "Nemesis of Faith" carried off far from that sheltered port, out upon the stormy sea, who was at last cast by the reflux into Carlyle's arms, to be healed by that apostle of agnostic stoicism, but so imperfectly healed as to have made of the work of his life —his "History of England in the Sixteenth Century" —a gigantic diatribe against Catholicism. Such, in fine, was Mark Pattison, who died as rector of Lincoln College, Oxford, a soured, or rather withered soul, still less on account of the miscalculations or the delays of his university ambition than by reason of his great spiritual mishap—that public coach not being at hand to bring him to abjure Protestantism along with his master, and, by the same chance, failing him all his life, his falling into systematic doubt, into malicious

erudition after the manner of Bayle, into haughty criticism and superfine irony like Renan's—with those
"Memoirs," as the chief work of that long life of studious leisure, in which he has traced the darkest, the
most melancholy, the most harrowing picture of a
dried-up intellect, of an arid heart, voluntarily shriv-
eled and yet forever inconsolable on account of the
ideal formerly glimpsed at, half possessed, lost forever.

It is to this rich gallery that Mr. Purcell has just
added as an authorized contribution the two massive
volumes of his biography of Manning. This work was
awaited with impatience. It was given out that the
Cardinal, in the closing years of his life, had opened
his secret treasures and his archives to this writer. To
a certain extent, an authorized biography was spoken
of, and the executors of Manning's will did not think
that they could, after his death, show themselves more
greedy or more timid than he: they let Mr. Purcell
pillage at will among the deceased's most secret papers.
Well! this book, compiled under such favorable
auspices, is not merely a bad book, it is a bad action.
Manning's successor, Cardinal Vaughan, and the testa-
mentary executors, have indignantly protested against
this publication. Though Mr. Purcell tries to defend
himself, and though he finds supporters among those
small minds whose greatest joy it is to see every greatness lowered, he has every impartial reader against
him. One must have read him in order to know how
far lack of style, disconnectedness, and, in a sense,
systematic disorder can go. His book is filled with
scraps of letters and of diaries, cut up into fragments,

into crumbs, scattered at random, transposed without
the least regard to chronology and association of ideas.
It sometimes resembles a manuscript whose pages, cast
here and there by the wind, had been sown together by
an illiterate servant girl, sometimes a paper basket up-
set on a table. What are we to say of the innumerable
errors that enamel almost every page and that give
every reason to be surprised at an English writer, a
Catholic, who had devoted years to these studies? To
imagine that the emancipation of the Catholics was still
on the order of the day in 1830; to persist in calling
the Tractarians *Puseyites* before 1835, at a time when
Pusey had scarcely given his valuable adhesion to Newman publicly, and when he had the honor of attaching
his name to his party only after 1845; to betray in
every word an inconceivable ignorance of Oxford, and
of the affairs and the men of the University; to be
scarcely able to touch on a point of the history of
Anglo-Catholicism, or even of the general, religious or
political history of England, without getting lost in a
labyrinth of inaccuracies and contradictions; to go out
of his way in dishonoring Latin quotations with gross
barbarisms; in fine, to write in a dull style, oscillating
between the emphatic and the commonplace—these are
some of Mr. Purcell's sins. They would be venial in
my estimation if they stood alone. The inexcusable
thing is, that a man to whom Manning had opened the
most secret registers of his papers and of his heart, who
lived in familiar, intimate intercourse with a great soul,
takes it upon himself as a mission to interlard his extracts and his summaries with outrageous commentaries

and perfidious insinuations; that he systematically gives an unfavorable interpretation to all the words, all the acts, all the silences of his hero; that he gratuitously attributes to him egoism, ambition, jealousy, duplicity, love for and art in intrigue, nay even cowardice, and all equally morbid and ignoble; that he uses his own errors of fact or his gross confusion of ideas as a text upon which to calumniate him upon whom he pretends to pass judgment—that, it will be acknowledged, is something more than readers will imagine; that also, I think, is something that exceeds a biographer's right. Mr. Purcell, moreover, becomes so very unconscionable that he professes, perhaps sincerely, a great admiration for the man whom he has just treated in this way. His code of literary proprieties is also quite strange. In order to prove his gratitude to Mr. Gladstone, of old closely allied with Manning, and who lavished confidences and revelations on his friend's biographer, he dubs him in passing with the amiable surname of *Judas.* He entertained no scruple about publishing either letters expressly placed under the seal of the strictest confidence, or documents calculated to re-awaken old quarrels between the dead or to provoke new ones between the living.

Such an author rules himself out of court. It is not thus that one writes history. As to knowing whether he ought to have been prevented from causing this scandal, shall I dare to acknowledge to my shame that I am not free from rejoicing at some of the results of his indelicacy? *Felix culpa,* since, with whatever intention he has acted, Mr. Purcell, like Froude of old

with that realist and impressionist, Carlyle, who so
greatly shocked the Sage of Chelsea's friends, has given
us, in the fragmentary state, in absolute disorder, an
incomparable series of revelations, of original documents; a Manning painted by himself; involuntary
avowals, touches and retouches, the authentic confessions of a soul of the first rank. It is furthermore announced that, by way of refutation, the executors of
the Cardinal's will and his closest friends will ere long
publish an official version of his life. These posthumous controversies, however painful they may be,
often make the light shine. Even after Mr. Purcell's
rich, insolent and indiscreet reaping, with its badly
bound sheaves, there still remain indeed some ears to
be gleaned. In the meantime, we have already, besides some important review articles published after
Manning's death and a small work by Miss Harriet
King, in Mr. Hutton's modest little book a work from
which Mr. Purcell could have learned that, in order to
avoid the continuous panegyric of the lives of the saints
and the affecting colorings of the order of hagiography,
there is no need of indulging in satire or disparagement.

I.

It was in 1832 that Henry Edward Manning, then
twenty-four years old, presented himself for ordination
and entered the ranks of the Anglican clergy. His first
vocation did not call him to it. Born on July 15,
1808, the last child by the second marriage of a rich
merchant of the City of London, William Manning,
who sat in Parliament among the Tories, Henry Ed-

ward had indeed been intended by his parents for the clerical calling. The family, of good connections among the country gentry, was respectably religious; but this project had been inspired in Manning's parents much less by views of piety than by the desire and hope of procuring for their Benjamin a comfortable and safe living. The child himself did not show any taste for this profession. In the preparatory schools which he frequented, and at Harrow, to which he went at the age of fifteen, he was not a studious pupil. He distinguished himself more at cricket than in the school exercises. Yet these four years in one of the great public schools which, along with Eton, Rugby and Winchester, receive the pick of English youth, were not useless to him. Wellington was fond of saying that it was on the Eton school play-grounds that the victory of Waterloo had been won. In any case, there comes out of those establishments, and only therefrom, that special product known as the English *gentleman*. Manning was such all his life in the full meaning of the term. This indescribable quality was always lacking to Newman, his equal by birth, his superior in the gifts of the intellect, but who did not pass through one of those great schools.

In 1827, when his son left Harrow, William Manning's fortune was already impaired. A minimum of from twelve to fourteen hundred dollars a year was needed to provide for the young student's support at Oxford. The father hesitated, and Manning had to swear to make up for lost time and to go and take an intermediate course from a clergyman; and to his so-

6

journ at this man's house he ever afterwards attributed
the solidity of the foundations of his knowledge of the
classics and his success at Oxford.   At the age of
twenty he was matriculated in Balliol College.   Ambitious as he was,—he took for his motto, as we learn
from one of his letters: *Aut Cæsar aut nihil*,—he resolved
to stand abreast with the pick of his generation.   His
conscientious application found its reward.   In the
Michaelmas examinations (November, 1830) he won a
first class or the diploma of honor for the classical
studies to which he had confined his desires.   Nevertheless, it was in another direction that, during these
years at Oxford, he specially distinguished himself.

The Union, or conference of the students, had just
been founded.   That wrangling society, that parliament in miniature, which, along with its rival of Cambridge, has seen nearly all the eminent men of England
sit on its benches, had a modest and frugal beginning,
not in the sumptuous hall in which it now frequently
attracts to its oratorical jousts members of Parliament
and ministers of State, but in the contracted quarters
of the students.   Samuel Wilberforce, the son of the
great philanthropist, the future Anglican prelate,—
Golden-mouthed Samuel or *Soapy Sam*, according to the
point of view which one takes in order to appreciate
him,—had just vacated the presidency.   There William
Ewart Gladstone was about to serve his apprenticeship
in eloquence.   Manning spoke a great deal; he spoke
well; he spoke on all subjects *et de quibusdam aliis*, from
the great questions of general politics to the smallest
details of the interior of a household.

A witty and sharp pen, that of the late Lord Houghton, has described one of the most memorable days of
that time. Cambridge also had its Union, and, ever in
rivalry with Oxford, prided itself on its superiority
over the *barbarians* of the sister University. On the
banks of the Isis they were still admiring in Byron the
poet of the age and of youth, whilst on the banks of
the Cam, Shelley's more recent and more heterodox
renown had already eclipsed the name of the singer of
"Manfred" and of "Childe Harold." At the sugges-
tion of Arthur Hallam, the son of the historian, the
very youth on whom a premature death was to confer
immortality by giving to his friend Tennyson the
opportunity of erecting to his memory the monument
of "In Memoriam," a delegation of missionaries was
charged to go and cast defiance at the Oxford Byron-
ians in the name of the poet of "Prometheus Un-
bound" and of the "Epipsychidion." Hallam himself, Moncton Milnes, the future Lord Houghton, the
essayist and distinguished poet, and last, Sunderland,
one of those great men of twenty whom destiny pun-
ishes for their precociousness, went to plead this cause.
Gladstone served as introducer to the revolutionists.
The contest was epic and passionate, with those savory
exaggerations that are the charm and honor of youth.
No one will ever know which side won the victory. If
the majority gave their votes to Manning, the uncompromising defender of Byron, he declared later on that
the arguments of the trio of Shelleyites had *routed* him.

Those fine times of disinterested study, of generous
enthusiasm, of pure friendships, pass but too quickly.

It was necessary to enter upon practical life. Manning's vocation at this period was quite decided. Politics attracted him, took entire hold of him. He dreamt of Parliament, of oratorical successes, of power, of action. He already saw himself Prime Minister, and his Oxford comrades, if they had taken his horoscope and that of Gladstone, would have reserved the mitre and crozier for the latter and given the seals of State to the future Archbishop of Westminster. Fate decided otherwise. William Manning was a ruined man. He had had, with a broken heart, to close up his business, to send in his resignation as a regent of the Bank of England, of which he had even been governor for some time, and as a member of the House of Commons, and to sell his fine country-seat. It was not with the crumbs of the paternal patrimony that one could meet the expenses of a Parliamentary career, such as Manning dreamt of — after the English fashion, in which one gives his leisure and his revenues to the service of the country, instead of supporting himself or making his fortune in one of the services. Thus discouraged, from the careless patronage of Lord Goderich Manning had to accept a more than modest place of supernumerary in the Colonial office.

He was pressed to reflect, to adopt the calling of the Church rather than to enter the civil service by this low back door. He refused. His religious feelings were far from being intense. There were found in him none of those strange presentiments, of that congenital, almost morbid, mysticism, that hidden and ardent spiritual life, after the manner of St. Teresa, of that species of half-waking dream, the indelible picture of which has been left to us by Newman and which marked him in advance, as if by a miracle, in the very heart of Protestantism, for Catholicism and the priesthood. The awakening of the religious conscience, the *conversion*, if I may use the technical term of Protestant psychology, was brought about in Manning by a feminine influence. He was connected with a great banking family of the city, the Bevans. Miss Bevan was a thoroughly religious soul, profoundly impregnated with the piety and the theology of that school of Evangelicalism, whose influence I will have to characterize. She read the Bible, she prayed along with the young man; in short, she was the instrument which God made use of to touch that heart and to conquer that soul. This was only a beginning; we will see that Manning made his true and complete conversion date from his malady of 1847; but its germ was none the less planted.

It is interesting to note in passing that the two leaders of the English Catholic restoration, one as well as the other, owed to *Evangelicalism* — and one as well as the other so proclaimed — their birth into the spiritual life. Newman was for years a zealous adherent not only of the religious school, but of the ecclesiastical party of that name. He founded and directed for some time at Oxford one of the specific institutions of this form of Protestantism, an auxiliary committee of the Bible Society. He himself, in his "Apologia," in which he weighed each expression, has declared that he in a certain sense owed *his soul*—the phrase is a strong one—to Scott's arch-Protestant Bible commen-

tary. Manning also, even after his public adhesion to
the Oxford movement, remained in communion with
some of the chief members of the Evangelical party.
In that there is an important fact. These two cardinals,
these two athletes of Catholicism, not only began with
Protestantism, but with what was most Protestant in
Protestantism. Their own testimony assures us that
both of them preserved a memory, nay more, an indelible trace of it. Certainly, when they submitted to the
Church, and by that very act, they repudiated everything that in their eyes constituted the errors and the
sin of schism and heresy; but the experience of the
past in that regard none the less remained to them.
They knew, they knew personally, all the good, the
excellence, the truth, that a false system can conceal.
They knew, they knew of themselves, that even in
militant, irreconcilable Protestantism, however far from
entirely faithful to the Gospel and docile to Revelation
it may be, there is the germ of all the truths, including
those that it rejects and that form the crowning of
Catholicism. To them, certain methods of controversy
to which controversy on the Continent is too often lowered, were altogether impossible : they could not have
recourse to them without contradicting themselves and
calumniating their own past.

At that time, however, Manning had not yet come
to this. He had just received the spark that was to
light in him, never again to be extinguished, the sacred
fire of the mind. His father's ruin, with all that it
entailed for him, was the first call to a higher vocation.
A secret sorrow—a prudent father's refusal to authorize

the union, more dreamt of than solicited, of a young
supernumerary in the Colonial office with his daughter
—came to complete the work that had been begun.
The voices from on high gained the upper hand. He
has himself described, in a letter of that period to his
confidential friend, his brother-in-law, the sickly, wild,
soured, enraged, indolent, ill-at-ease condition of his
soul; his need of being anywhere else than where he
was, of doing, of hearing everything else than what he
was doing or hearing; in a word, of being everything
else than what he was: a coarse, stupid, monstrous
body, some creature or other. His melancholy sometimes degenerated into a sort of skeptical cynicism:
Everything is false, soul or body, mechanism or clap-
trap. Ah! philosophy! let us speak of it: *Vitæ magis-
tra, doctrinarum excultrix, artium indagatrix, etc.* Yes,
truly, when everything is nice and quite warm and
comfortable, oh! then it is the most faithful of friends,
the best of companions, of counselors, of consolers, of
protectors. But when things assume a mean aspect,
well! there it is gone, its tail in the air, like a cow too
well fed, in a time of storm. It was only a well-known
form of the malady of growth: an acute attack of
Byronism or of Wertherism, complicated with a too
natural discouragement at the sight of that world, all
of whose avenues were shut against the hopes or the
ambitions of his twenty-five years.

Manning knew later on how to discern the Providential
hand that was inflicting all these deceptions upon him
at the very hour when an internal travail had begun in
his soul, the voice that was speaking to him a language

so clear and so exalted. He resolved, and it is he himself who tells us so, not to become a clergyman in the sense dreamt of by his father, but to renounce the world and to live for God and for souls. And he adds that he had prayed a great deal, had much frequented the churches. It was the turning point of his life. I pity those who, like Mr. Purcell and certain of his critics, see only a sort of last shift and of purely mundane speculation in the determination that could be traced by Manning himself in these words so simple and so beautiful: It was an appeal from God quite as clearly as any one of those that He afterwards addressed to him, an appeal *ad veritatem et ad seipsum.*

The proof that he was not obeying purely human motives is, as he has noted, that the mere thought of being a clergyman was of itself odious to him. He says that he had a veritable antipathy against the secular character, the worldliness of the Established Church. The sight of the stock and cap (insignia of the Anglican bishops) literally put him beside himself. The title, father in God, applied to bishops living in comfort, keenly irritated him. His only thought was to obey God's will, to save his soul and the souls of others.

Manning had the good fortune of having been placed from the beginning in an extremely favorable position. Scarcely had he been ordained by the Bishop of Oxford, after the ludicrous preparation that sufficed at that time for the Anglican clergy, when he became, in January, 1833, one of the vicars under the Reverend John Sargent, rector of Lavington and lord of the manor, his

relative by marriage. The eldest daughter of the
family had already married Samuel Wilberforce, the
future bishop, recently appointed rector of a parish in
the Isle of Wight. It was the destiny of these girls to
reward the zeal of their father's youthful assistants. A
few months had scarcely elapsed when the youngest of
them, Caroline, became Manning's wife. Since the
month of May, Manning, on the death of his intended
father-in-law, had been entrusted by his betrothed's
grandmother, who reigned at the castle and owned the
right of presentation, in charge of this important
parish. At twenty-five, after an apprenticeship of
scarcely more than a few weeks, Manning found himself in the position of a beneficed priest, which so many
members of the clergy never reach. Married, with a
competent income, in a high station, he was in a most
enviable position.

This very good fortune had its dangers. Who
knows, in case it should have been prolonged, whether
the rector of Lavington, the husband of an accomplished woman, perhaps surrounded by children, in
possession of a handsome revenue, at the head of an
important parish, on the road to dignities, would not
gradually have fallen to the level of that comfortable,
respectable, honest, kindly, well incomed, well fed
clergy which necessarily furnishes good fathers of
families, few ascetics or saints, and which believes
more in the wise precepts of orthodox political economy
than in the divine folly of charity? God preserved
him from this danger. He left to him the shell of his
happiness, that eminent position, that luxury, those

horses that he loved and in the knowledge of which he
excelled, all that external decoration which Manning
himself repelled with a firm hand as soon as he had
taken his first steps on the way of renunciation; but He
struck him straight to the heart.

After four years of cloudless felicity, his wife was
taken from him. Manning has not allowed any one to
fathom his sorrow. There are feelings too sacred for a
man to speak of them. Manning was never one of
those who profane the secrecy of their memories, who
make a public place of the sanctuary of their affections,
who retail their heart in slices. Never, even again in
the service of a Church which allows its ministers to
marry, did he make a direct allusion to his loss, even
in his correspondence with those closest to him, even
in his secret diary. He briefly refers to this date—
July 24, 1837—only in the list of the charitable dis-
pensations by which God led him to Himself. Later
on, other reasons came to seal his silence still more
hermetically. As a Catholic priest, as the head of a
clergy vowed to celibacy, it was not agreeable to him to
reawaken this memory.

Others took charge of it for him, if we are to believe
a legend that is perhaps devoid of authenticity. During the vehement, and sometimes envenomed, struggles
that he had to maintain against certain factions in the
fold of Catholicism, an old priest, who detested the new
regime, was accustomed to celebrate as a day of mourning the anniversary of Mrs. Manning's death, and, when
he was asked the reason for it, he answered that it was
the date of the severest blow that God in our time had

inflicted on the Church in the British Isles.* Even as
a married man, however, Manning had not slept in
happiness. Side by side with an indefatigable parish
activity, he was not slow to take his stand on the battle-
ground of the struggle that was absorbing every mind.

II.

It was a solemn hour when the Oxford movement
broke out with a din of war. The Established Church
of England, by reason of the strange anomalies of its
beginnings, had always concealed within it the germs
of two contradictory systems, namely, Catholicism and
Protestantism. The struggle between these two opposing elements disturbed the entire first half of the seventeenth century. Archbishop Laud was an Anglo-
Catholic before his time. He contracted a fatal alliance
with that fatal dynasty of the Stuarts, and he expiated
on the scaffold still less his hostility against triumphant
Puritanism than his complicity with Strafford and
Charles I. in their abortive attempt at absolute government, without Parliament. Anglican theology, with
Hooker, with Bull, with those non-jurors who were
wrong in erecting into a dogma the purely human and
political doctrine of legitimacy and of non-resistance,

* Mr. Purcell, in a note on p. 310 of this volume, relates that,
some one having said that Newman's conversion was the greatest
calamity that the Catholic Church has suffered in our day, Canon
MacMullen answered in the negative, saying that the greatest mis-
fortune to the Church of our day was the death of a woman (Mrs.
Manning). I have personal reasons for not putting too implicit
faith in this anecdote, and especially in a pretended subsequent
dialogue between the Cardinal and the Canon.

none the less continued to repudiate Protestantism and
its inspirations. In the eighteenth century, however,
with the definitive victory of the revolution of 1688 and
the accession of the house of Hanover, it is the domi-
nance of all the powers of spiritual death, of Erastian-
ism or of the absolute subordination of the Church to
the State ; of practical materialism, of formalism, of
rationalism ; of that shameful Christianity which is
afraid of its shadow, which dreads and proscribes nothing so much as enthusiasm, which is reduced to a
purely civil morality and observes a cowardly silence
on revealed dogma. It was, properly speaking, the
sleep of death.

A reawakening of faith, of zeal, of ardor, of generous
imprudence, was at last brought about. It took place
outside the Anglican Church. John Wesley remained,
indeed, until the end its faithful and devoted son. If
he founded a new sect, Methodism, whose adherents
are now counted by millions in the English-speaking
world, it was in spite of him, against his personal resistance. He had wanted to touch consciences, to save
souls, to preach the eternal Gospel; thanks to Anglican
intolerance, he found that he had created a Church.
The beginnings of primitive Methodism had something
of the grandeur, of the simplicity of nascent Christianity, or, if this comparison shocks, of the foundation of
the mendicant orders. Its apostles knew how to make
the basic chords of the sentiment of sin and of repent-
ance vibrate in the souls of the people, ever accessible
to these great simple emotions. The counter-blast to
this powerful movement made itself felt even in the

Anglican Church. Methodism and Wesley were the authors of that beneficent reaction of Evangelicalism which restored some religious sap to the Anglican establishment.

Among the products of Protestantism there is none more authentic than Evangelicalism. Therein were its grandeurs and its littlenesses, its qualities and its defects. Strictly individualist, it especially appealed to the emotions of religious sensibility. The great affair to it was conversion, looked at, not as the slow and progressive action of the Spirit of God, operating through all the ordinary and extraordinary channels of grace on a human creature, but as an indivisible point in time and space, the sudden transformation of a soul, the miraculous and instantaneous deliverance which breaks the yoke of sin. From the beginning, in spite of the great things that were done or that were provoked by the new school, and to which M. de Rémusat, formerly and in this very place, paid eloquent homage, people had to acknowledge that it presented grave and fatal defects. It lacked the meaning of penance in the tragic sense which this word bore to an Augustine, a Saint-Cyran or a Pascal. There was wanting to it the notion of the Church, the conception of the sacraments, the consciousness of human solidarity and of divine authority. There was wanting to it, in fine, a theology, the understanding of dogma and of the place that belongs to it in a supernatural and revealed religion.

These defects, however, became noticeable only in time. In the first instance, Evangelicalism showed itself as a power of life and progress. A divine breath joined again and reanimated the scattered bones of Anglican formalism. The clergy ceased, according to the witty and too just remark of Joseph de Maistre, to be a company of gentlemen clad in black who retailed honest things from the pulpit on Sunday. The clergyman, described by Macaulay, not without a trifle of exaggeration, as the humble parasite of the rural manors, the intended husband of My Lady's ex-chambermaid or, worse than that, of My Lord's discarded mistress,—Fielding's parson, the eater of the family leavings, a lettered Bohemian or a poor village pastor with just a bare living,—even the rectors and the curates, so admirably pictured in their romances by Jane Austen and later on by George Eliot, those joyous and robust country gentlemen, always the first at the hunting meet, better initiated in the mysteries of sport or of the turf than in those of theology, all that old-regime clergy began, like an antediluvian fauna, to disappear under the influence of Evangelicalism.

There the reaction did not stop. The laity were even more affected by it. A splendid impulse was given to the great undertakings of charity and philanthropy. It will be to the eternal honor of that doctrine which, by its narrow conception of salvation by faith, seemed destined to paralyze all religious activity, that it made a whole harvest of Christian works spring up: missions among pagans, at last cleansing Protestantism of the reproach of neglecting one of Christ's commandments; committees on aid, on popular instruction, on penal reform; especially that admirable movement against slavery and the slave trade with which the name of Wilberforce is connected.

Such is the balance sheet of Evangelicalism. It has left indelible traces, not only on the history, but on the moral and intellectual constitution of the English people. Towards the end of the first quarter of this century, it was in the zenith of power and success. The heroic age had passed. That great current of enthusiasm was in the act of being controlled, directed and solidified. In its turn, victorious Evangelicalism, caressed and professed by those who but lately were persecuting it, ran the risk of becoming a Pharisaism. It fell back into formalism, but into a formalism a hundred times worse, because the affectation of certain sentiments made a hypocrisy of it and because it lacked, as a compensation, the ample traditions, the broad perspectives, the intrinsic solidity of the sacraments of the Anglo-Catholic system.

It was precisely the period when the progress of Liberalism seemed to put, if not the Church, at least the ecclesiastical establishment, in peril. In the order of thought and of knowledge, after the philosophy of the eighteenth century and its popular rationalism, people were already witnessing the first attempts of the higher criticism,—of that German criticism with which Pusey went to come in contact on that university pilgrimage from which he brought back such a curious book. In the political order, the hour was approaching for the triumph of the Whigs after half a century of Tory government, and of extreme resistance to every novelty in spirituals as well as in temporals. The spirit of tolerance, erroneously confounded with the spirit of skeptical indifference, thanks to the *great treason* of Peel and

Wellington, had just won a decisive victory in the matter of Catholic emancipation and was going to abolish the Tests or religious oaths. The Liberals openly avowed their design of reforming the Church, of suppressing bishoprics and prebends, of revising revenues and endowments, and of abolishing tithes. A voice coming from a very exalted station had just summoned the bishops to put their house in order. In fine, the accession of new layers of those middle classes, entirely permeated with the leprosy of Nonconformity, the growing shadow cast on the insular kingdom by the continental revolution, were all frightening the faithful. The younger clergy, in particular, felt themselves summoned to a holy war.

These champions cast their eyes all around them in order to discover means of defence. In the official arsenal of Anglicanism they found only rusty, mossgrown, worn-out weapons of the State religion and of political orthodoxy. As regards Evangelicalism, on the one side, it bargained with the enemy by communicating with the schismatics of Protestant dissent; on the other, it offered only imperfectly tempered weapons, which flew to pieces at the first contact with the refined and double-edged blades of Catholic controversy or revolutionary polemics. If the Church of England was to be saved, it was necessary to find its titles again and to give them back to it. If it was to be put in shelter from human enterprise, it was necessary to restore to it the supernatural powers of its divine mission. If it was anything else than the creature of the State, at the mercy of the holders of temporal power, it was neces-

sary to restore its spiritual power, to turn it back to its
supernatural beginnings and to bring again into light
those *notes* or those authentic characters which are in-
herent in the Church and without which there is no
Church. The whole Oxford movement, Anglo-Catholicism in its entirety, was in germ in the perception of
these needs.

A few young men, for the most part connected with
Oriel College, Oxford, felt themselves pressed to enter
the field. Keble, formerly famous for a university
career of unequaled brilliancy, retired in a country parish, not without a ray of glory having come to seek him
there after the publication of his poem, "The Christian
Year," of a poesy that was somewhat arch, but yet sincere and fresh, had just preached (July 14, 1833), at
the opening of the Oxford sessions, that sermon on
national apostasy in which Newman always saw the
first clarion call of the holy war. Newman had arrived
from that journey in Italy and Sicily, quite illuminated
with mysterious presentiments, quite gloomy from superstitious fears, a journey that came near ending in
the tomb. He had come in contact, not without the
unaffected fear and the scruples of a child brought up
in another sanctuary, with the religion of the Catholic
world. He returned from it with the still vague intuition of a great mission, with the zeal of a renewed con-
consecration.

Among the friends to whom he revealed these secret
thoughts, Richard Hurrell Froude exerted on him the
most decisive influence. Already suffering from the
phthisis that was to carry him off, he had the somewhat

7

feverish impetuosity of a man whose days are numbered. Brought up in the purest traditions of the High Church by his father, the Archdeacon, he had gathered in a few morsels of the Anglo-Catholic heritage of these two precursors, Alexander Knox and Bishop Jebb. In order to bring himself nearer to the Catholic Church, he had an infinitely shorter road to travel than the Protestant Newman, a descendant through his mother of Huguenot refugees and brought up in the atmosphere of Evangelicalism. Newman at this date still saw in Rome the *great prostitute* of the Apocalypse and in the Pope Antichrist. His imagination, saturated with the metaphors of Protestant controversy, persisted in suggesting to him those grotesque analogies, even when his reason and his conscience had brought him closer to Catholicism. In the beginning of his work, when he commenced the publication of the "Tracts for the Times," he was totally exempt from every predilection for Rome, even of the most secret character. Quite the contrary, he combated in it the great enemy that was compromising truth, every time that it did not corrupt it, and whose systematic undertakings, superfœtations and usurpations explained, if they did not justify, the errors, mutilations and negations of Protestantism.

Leaning his back against his, to him, invincible theory of conformity with the primitive Church and of the immutable deposit of faith, Newman was by no means afraid to hurl defiance at those two formidable powers, Catholicism and Protestantism. Not only did he deem it possible to find between these two forms of error a *via media*, equally distinct from each of them, but in his estimation the Anglican Church was alone in possession of the monopoly of truth and of the whole truth. Strange and noble illusion of a thoroughly intellectualist genius! Newman had gone out in search of the best means of defence for the Church that was dear to him, and he had concluded that the safest, as well as the simplest, was to claim for it the supernatural characteristics of the Church in itself. To postulate for a purely national and insular Church, separated from the rest of the world, subject to the civil authority, thoroughly penetrated with the doctrines and rites of the Reformation—to postulate for it the *notes* of the Church, one, eternal, immutable, infallible, visible—that is to say, according to Vincent of Lerins' formula, the *semper* . . . , *ubique* . . . , *ab omnibus*—such was the desperate undertaking or pledge to which, one fine day in the year of grace 1833, a young and obscure Fellow of Oriel devoted himself. On this foundation he built the edifice of the "Tracts for the Times," of those small periodical pamphlets of which he was always the inspirer, the reviser and the responsible editor, and most frequently the author.

These leaflets were prodigiously successful. From to-day until to-morrow a great party was formed. Newman was its leader. He was famous, he was powerful. He was entering upon that extraordinary phase of his life which lasted twelve years and whose steps he himself noted as those of a way of the cross. To England was presented the unprecedented sight of a mere ecclesiastic, without dignity, without rank in the hierarchy, becoming the generalissimo of a great army, the absolute master of a troop of devoted friends, the infallible oracle of a school, the director of the consciences of a multitude of penitents.   It has been said that at that period, as regards many men of eminence, endowed with reason and will, the adequate and complete formula of their faith was : *Credo in Newmanum.* His sermons at St. Mary's, the parish church of the University, were attended by immense audiences.   His modest rooms at Oriel were a sanctuary whose threshold was not crossed without emotion.   A word from him, nay less than that, a fugitive shadow of an expression, a gesture, a silence, were listened to, obeyed, as the commands of an absolute king or the decrees of an infallible pontiff.   Rarely has a man, either in this age or in any age, more completely tasted the intoxicating joys of an intellectual and moral dictatorship.

What is most emotional and pathetic in his case is that, for nearly all that time, the object of this adoration, the idol of this worship, is a prey to the poignant anguish of doubt.   He sees opening beneath his feet the very ground on which he is building that imposing edifice.   He sees abysses gaping on all sides of him, and, more unfortunate than Pascal, it is he himself who leads thither to be lost all those who have confidence in him.   His logic has taken hold of him in a pitiless vise.   It carries him, from deduction to deduction, to starting from premises that he has laid down and that the unknowing multitude acclaim, to conclusions in the presence of which his whole soul recedes in terror, which it hates, which are the overturning of his work, but from which he cannot in good faith withdraw.

Newman has left us in his "Apologia," and in a
more direct and still more palpitating form in his
"Letters," the history of that soul adventure. Rather
early did he feel that he did not have the right to limit
his assertions precisely to whatever they could contain
that was useful to his cause. It would have been too
advantageous, and not honest enough, to amputate his
theories from all that exceeded the current conception
of Anglicanism, to curtail all that menaced the pretentions or revealed the contradictions of the Church of
England. Accepting and invoking a part of the formula of St. Vincent of Lerins, he could not in good
conscience reject any of it without condemning the rest.
Did not his doctrine of the rule of Christian antiquity,
of conformity to the primitive Church, logically imply
Catholicism? How were people to assert in the same
breath that the Church is the depository and interpreter
of revealed truth by right divine, and that she is the
mistress of errors and the godmother of popular super-
stitions? By what right should people proclaim the
infallible Church of the first three centuries, of the
great œcumenical councils, in order to arrive at the
conclusion of the great defection of the Church in the
Middle Ages, at the straying of the Council of Trent?

The fright with which Newman saw these questions
arise was sincere. If his mind began to throw off the
yoke of his Protestant prejudices, his heart and his
imagination were still enslaved to them. In his presence still arose this dilemma: to continue to build, on
the foundations that he had laid, amid songs of
triumph and exclamations of joy, the majestic Angli-

can cathedral,—but then to go to the end, to crown its summit with the cross of St. Peter and to submit to Rome;—or, indeed, firmly to reject the Papal pretensions, to repudiate unflinchingly the extreme consequences of the Catholic system,—but then to acknowledge openly the midway theory of the *via media* was wrong, that the whole Tractarian undertaking had set out from a false starting point and that Geneva was right. It is easy to take account of what was to be tragical in the condition of the head of a party, devoured by those thoughts at the very moment and partly because of its successes.

To Newman, thrown back upon himself, absorbed in those inner struggles, it seemed that he was fated to strike a mortal blow at the Church, his mother, whether he abandoned it to go and kneel at the feet of his haughty enemy, or snatched from it with his own hands the royal crown that he had just placed on its head. So much filial piety necessarily ending in an act of parricide! This internal work was already far advanced when, in addition, a whole series of external facts, of positive, undeniable events, came to show him all that was imaginary, fictitious, contrary to reality, in his fundamental assertions. There was no longer question of knowing theoretically whether a Church which possesses—or which claims—a part of the supernatural attributes of the ideal Church has the right, in good logic, to repudiate the others. To Newman there was question of shutting his eyes to the evidence of the facts or to draw from them their inevitable conclusions.

In spite of the almost miraculous propagation of his

doctrines, or rather by reason of that very diffusion which provoked conflicts and gave rise to opposition, Newman had to show that Anglicanism did not possess the distinctive signs of the Church of God. Those fictions of an inspired witness of revelation, of an inviolable depository of dogma, of a faithful administrator of the sacraments, of an episcopate in the direct line of the Apostolic succession—with what face were they to be maintained when all the facts belied them? when the Anglican Church suffered and accepted the nomination of a heretic—Hampden—as Regius professor of theology? when it took active steps only to condemn baptismal regeneration, preached too strictly by Pusey, or the too Catholic system of interpretation of Tract No. 90, or the impetuous Ward and his *ideal Church?* when the episcopate gave over to the civil power the keys of the citadel, recovered energy only to fire on its own troops and to rage against the too zealous faithful?

From that time, and it is he himself who has said it, Newman is on his deathbed. For five years more he prolongs his agony; he stiffens against the call that is urging him to the feet of the Vicar of Jesus Christ. His old instincts, his education, sorrow at himself overthrowing the work of his life; the mortification of apparently justifying by a supreme act the odious calumnies that accused him of Jesuitically masking his real design and of deliberately, with premeditation, doing the work of Catholicism; the ties of family and of friendship, the fear of scandalizing faithful hearts and docile minds; the memory of the graces received in the communion of the Anglican Church; that filial piety

which is not extinguished in a day, even when you
have learned that the mother who carries you in her
arms is not your true mother—all these feelings together
were boiling in him, were torturing him, were holding
him back.

To justify this obstinate resistance in his own estimation, he took refuge in the most desperate, nay even
the most sophistical, expedients. At one time he found
some consolation in the mystical theory of the *Babylon-
ian Captivity*. In his estimation the Anglican Church
was sick, a slave to the civil power, a prey to error;
but the duty of those who were born in it was none
the less to live and to die in its bosom, that is to say,
in privation of the graces granted to more favored com-
munions, but with the keen satisfaction of obedience
until the end and of fidelity in spite of everything.
This ingenious expedient ceased to satisfy him on the
day when he made up his mind that, by this movement, he was but simply returning to Protestant individualism and to the suppression of the Church as a
means of grace. In reality his decision was taken when
he clearly perceived that he was held back, less by the
scruples of his conscience, the doubts of his reason or
the affections of his heart, than by the apprehensions of
the head of a party, the weariness of the humiliated
teacher, the point of honor of the general compelled to
pass over to the enemy.

One after another had he untied the bonds that held
him to the past. He ceased to reside at Oriel College;
he resigned his charge of the University parish of St.
Mary's; by order of his bishop he had interrupted the

series of the "Tracts for the Times"; he gave up the editing of his review, the *British Critic*. In fine, he retired to Littlemore, a hamlet near Oxford, into a sort of hermitage or modest convent which he had built and where, surrounded by a cohort of young disciples, he led for two or three years a cloistered and monkish life.

Events came hurriedly. Bunsen, the Prussian ambassador, gave, without knowing it, the last impulse to a slowly formed resolve, by obtaining the assent of the Government and of the Church of England to his favorite project of the creation of a mixed bishopric, half Anglican half Prussian, at Jerusalem. It was the patent, avowed coöperation, almost fusion with Continental Protestantism. In the autumn of 1845 the long agony came to its end. On October 8, Newman went to abjure Protestantism, to have himself received into the Catholic Church and to take communion from the hands of an Italian Passionist Father, then on a visit to England, from a former shepherd of the Roman Campagna, Father Dominick.

III.

I have had to follow the Oxford movement down to the final catastrophe. The mere fact that I could give an account of it without naming Manning even once clearly proves that, though he deeply felt its influence, he did not play any considerable part in that phase of it. The truth is that Newman is Tractarianism all by himself. Neither Manning's temperament, nor the circumstances of his life at that time, predisposed him

to take a leading part in the Anglo-Catholic movement
in its beginnings.   He was always much less a man of
retirement, a theorist, a theologian and an author, than
a man of action and of authority.   The diocese of
Chichester, thoroughly rural, in which for eighteen
years he exercised his parochial functions under four
bishops, only one of whom felt any sympathy for the
new ideas, was not Oxford.

Nevertheless, Manning was not slow, through the
intermediation of common friends, to come into relation with Newman.   The principles of the new school
appealed to every side of his nature.   Detached ere
long from the Evangelical party, he enrolled himself in
that of the Anglo-Catholics.   The first sermon that he
published was the official proclamation of this.   In it
he treated of the *rule of faith;* and its fundamental
affirmations, its developments, and especially the notes
with which he enriched it, bore the mark of the new
doctrine and the trace of the fact that he had submitted
the proofs of his work to Newman.   The Evangelicals
were moved.   Their organ, the *Record,*—a Protestant
Univers minus the talent,—inflicted a severe reprimand
on this new wolf in sheep's clothing.   The bishop of
Chester issued a diatribe against him.   Manning had
taken rank among the Tractarians.

All his friendships bore him to that side.   After
Robert Wilberforce, perhaps the closest of his friends,
who thought exactly as he did, and Henry Wilberforce,
his brother-in-law, he had scarcely any close connection but with Mr. Gladstone, then a young member of
the House of Commons, *the hope of uncompromising young*

Toryism, as Macaulay called him in an article on the great work that he had just published on the "Union of Church and State." On a journey to Rome, in 1838,—the first of the innumerable visits that Manning made to the Eternal City,—he had the young statesman for his companion. Together they went to see Dr. Wiseman, who scarcely suspected that he had before his eyes, in the person of this Anglican ecclesiastic, his successor on the as yet uncreated archiepiscopal throne of Westminster. Together they frequented the churches and heard a Father of the order of Friars Preachers whose sermon, popular and dogmatic at the same time, moved Mr. Gladstone to jealousy for Anglicanism. Together they were walking one fine Sunday on the *Piazza de Fiore* when the rector of Lavington, more strict on this point as an Anglican than he was later on as a cardinal of Holy Church, severely reproved Mr. Gladstone for the grave fault of having bought apples on the Sabbath day.

On returning to his parish, Manning, in spite of the accession of a bishop far from prejudiced in his favor, received in 1840—at the age of thirty-two—his promotion to the important post of Archdeacon of Chichester, one of the two lieutenants of the Ordinary in the directing of his clergy. It was the moment when, in the Tractarian camp, Newman in spite of himself betrayed his inner struggle, and when a whole band of bold young men, with Ward at their head, noisily proclaimed their contempt for the Reformation and their love for Catholicism. Manning had always been more Protestant than his Oxford ally. Never had it cost him anything, while professing the principles of the new school, to pay homage or do justice to those Reformers of the sixteenth century whose name seemed to scorch the mouth of certain Tractarians and whom Ward unhesitatingly consigned to eternal flames.

In reality, between Newman and Manning, even in that honeymoon of their relations, and again when later on Manning as a Catholic thought he ought to dedicate a book to Newman as the master to whom he owed more gratitude than to any other man, there never was full harmony or absolute sympathy. As long as they were both Protestants, Newman was by far the more Catholic of the two. I know a cumbrous as well as a simple way of explaining this mystery. It is the one naturally adopted by Mr. Purcell, ever on the lookout for whatever can belittle his hero. To him there can be no doubt but that Manning, a servant to fortune, an adorer of the rising sun, an enemy of lost causes (I am quoting my author), always took his stand on the side that he thought the stronger and howled with the wolves at Geneva as well as at Rome. This elegant solution of the problem presents, among other defects, that of leaving Newman's conduct without the slightest explanation, Newman taking the same direction as Manning, but for an opposite reason. The right key seems to me to be given by the contrast between these two natures.

The one is the very type of the intellectualist, struggling with his own conceptions, I almost said with the phantoms of his mind, led, from scruple and from subtlety, to call into question what is attracting him, to be distrustful of his own postulates, to saw off the branch

on which he is seated. The other is, in the full force
of the term, a man of action to whom ideas are not the
stakes of an infinitely subtle and complicated game, but
bases of operations, the foundations on which it is necessary to build. As the former will necessarily be inclined
to turn his *credo* over and over again and to look at it
in all its aspects, to seek for its weak points with uneasiness, to see especially the hollows and crevices of
the ground on which he has taken his stand, so the
second, from a need for certitude, from practical necessity, will be faithful to his premises and will go direct
to their logical conclusions. His Protestantism will be,
in its time, as robust as, later on, his Catholicism, and
both in their succession will be equally sincere.

It was indeed from conviction, and not from politics,
that at this time Manning was infinitely more anti-
Roman than most of his allies. He wrote to Pusey to
thank him for a work, but especially for the passages in
it that were most opposed to Rome. He added that his
conscience was stung at the thought of that turning
away of affection, of that sacrilegious transport of men's
hearts, of the mere object of worship to the Virgin Mary.
In his estimation, a letter from Dr. Wiseman that had
recently appeared sufficed to condemn the whole Catholic system; his parallel between the feelings of a child
for its mother and those of the faithful for the Virgin
to him seemed "dreadful." He differed radically in
his tone and in his language in regard to Catholicism,
not only from the light-weights of the party, but from
the grave doctors, from those who, like Pusey, were to
remain Anglicans to the end.

In 1844, to free his responsibility from what he con-
sidered the lax casuistry of Tract No. 90, he accepted
the task of preaching before the University, on November 5,—that is to say, the anniversary of the Gun-
powder Plot and of the landing of William of Orange
in 1688,—a sermon in honor of this double Protestant
jubilee. Some have sought to see a cowardly defection
in this act. It was only the honest application of his
principles. If Manning had not been able to call himself and to feel himself a Protestant and to take part in
the Protestant celebrations of his Church, he would not
have remained a single day in a communion that is
Protestant of right and in fact. Some of his friends
had a strong grudge against him for this manifestation
of it. Newman, to whom he went next day to pay a
visit at Littlemore, is said to have slammed the door in
his face, if we are to believe a rather suspicious legend,
since their correspondence was never interrupted and
since the rector of Lavington was one of the small number of those to whom Father Dominick's neophyte
communicated his final resolve.

So much, moreover, was he held to be one of the
champions of Anglo-Catholicism that adversaries made
no difference between him and the extreme Catholic-
izers. As some one announced Manning's journey to
Rome to the bishop of London, Blomfield: "To
Rome?" remarked the prelate; "I thought he had
been there already since the publication of his sermon."
These suspicions and the bickerings of the Evangelical
party hardly shackled the archdeacon of Chichester's
activity. His charges or annual instructions amply

and authoritatively treated of all the great questions
then under discussion. The "Essay on the Unity of
the Church," published in 1842 and dedicated to Mr.
Gladstone, was at once put in the rank of the classics
of Anglicanism. The bishop of Exeter, the famous
Phillpost, said: "We have three men on whom to
count: in the State, Gladstone; at the bar, Hope (Sir
Walter Scott's grandson-in-law, ere long a companion
of Manning's in conversion); in the Church, Manning;"
and he added: "There is no power in the world that
can keep Manning from becoming a bishop." A great
religious newspaper, the *Christian Remembrancer*, shared
this opinion and declared that the young archdeacon
was one of those men whom the Church needs in its
highest dignities and who could not grow old in the
honorable post that they occupy. At Littlemore, in
Newman's surroundings, on the eve of his submission,
they were equally convinced, as we know from the
testimony of Father Lockhart, then still an Anglican,
that Manning was designated for the episcopate. An
adversary, the eminent leader of the liberal party and
of Anglican rationalism, Frederick Denison Maurice,
after a brief sojourn under the same roof, in 1843, exclaimed that he did not know where, in his time, one
could find a better and a wiser bishop. Some years
later, after an important meeting, he wrote that there
was in that room a man who could save the Church, if
he wished, and that man was Manning. He himself,
in his secret diary, acknowledged to himself that he
had his foot on the last step of the ladder which he had
so much desired.

And so, when the crisis broke out, when Newman, by his conversion, that inexplicable event, according to Lord John Russell, inflicted, as Disraeli expressed it, a shock on England from which she is still trembling, when from day to day, from week to week, people learned of the defection of Ward, of Dalgairns, of Oakley, of nearly all the aides-de-camp of the recluse of Littlemore, the eyes of all, friends and enemies alike, were instinctively turned towards Manning as well as towards Pusey. They seemed the appointed leaders of a new campaign in which there was question of passing from the offensive to the defensive, in which there no longer was need of brilliant and adventurous outpost soldiers, but of men of authority and of government. Manning was deeply affected. To Newman he had written a farewell letter in which, while assuring him that, if he knew words that could express his profound love for him, *without sullying his conscience*, he would willingly use them, and, while deploring that they could no longer meet, in this life, at the foot of the same altar, he hoped they would see each other in the next world.

He foresaw the gravity of the crisis. The day on which he had at Oxford assisted at the degradation of Ward by the University, he had turned towards Gladstone, and had said to him in an undertone: 'Αρχὴ ὠδίνων, that is the beginning of sorrows. He did not know how to prophesy so well. Whilst Gladstone, who had enough confidence in him to write that he was beginning to think that, on a subject of importance, he could not differ in opinion with him, wished that the clarion

would sound loud and clear, Manning was beginning to
be a prey to cruel uncertainties. A mysterious, a
providential destiny, for him as well as for Newman,
would have it that the hour of doubt should coincide
with that of triumph. If he had been able to keep
until the end the serene and absolute faith that made
him condemn Newman's conversion as a sin, and
stupefy Gladstone by attributing the submissions to
Rome to a want of truth common to all the deserters,
he would have been happier and stronger. Two days
after Newman's *great treason*, he could still assert to an
intimate friend that nothing in the world could shake
his faith in Christ's presence in the Anglican Church
and in the sacraments.

To a man of action, at the very hour when he is
called upon to defend the most sacred of causes, this
certainty is indispensable. The anguish of losing it
gradually was not spared him. He saw himself forced,
on the one hand, to state the unsolvable contradictions
between the theory of Anglo-Catholicism and the realities of Anglicanism. On the other hand, the constant
progress of his internal and spiritual life, of his ever
more and more mystic piety, of his pastoral zeal, of his
asceticism, of his holiness, created in him new needs to
which the Anglican Church could offer only illusory
and lying satisfactions, but which the Catholic Church
was fully in a measure to satiate. From 1846 he noted
in his diary that the Anglican Church, in his estimation, was sick organically and functionally; that, in the
former relation, it was separated from the universal
Church and from the Chair of Peter, subject without

8

appeal to the civil power, despoiled of the sacrament of
penance and of the daily sacrifice of the Eucharist, deprived of the minor orders and mutilated in its ritual;
that, from the second point of view, it no longer had
daily service, nor discipline, nor unity in devotion or
ritual, nor preparatory education for its clergy, nor
sacerdotal life in its bishops and its priests, nor a hold
on the popular conscience, nor faith in the mysteries of
the invisible world.

This formidable act of accusation Manning was going
to repeat incessantly for five long years.   He was going
to reproach his own Church with being wanting in antiquity, system, intelligibility, order, force, unity.   He
was going to deplore those dogmas on paper only, that
universally abandoned ritual, that clergy and those
laymen profoundly divided.   He was going to say in
a melancholy tone that though he was not a Roman
Catholic, yet he had ceased to be an Anglican.   He was
going to struggle against himself, incessantly taking up
the examination of conscience, asking himself if he was
not a butt for the tempter's artifices, if he ought not to
be distrustful of himself, to consider that those who
have remained until now in Anglicanism are more
humble than those who have left it.   At the same time,
he is compelled to note that nothing in Rome repels
him enough to keep him away, whilst nothing in Protestantism attracts him sufficiently to hold him back.

He exclaimed, in July, 1846, that the principal thing
was the attraction of Rome, which satisfied him completely, reason, feeling, his whole nature, whilst the
Anglican Church was only an almost, and yet it was

that almost only by reason of the supplements and
additions that were brought to it. He writes these
curious words, which are at the same time an implicit
protest and the avowal of an irresistible seduction.
The net was tightening its meshes arround him. A
little later he felt as if a great light had shone in his
eyes. His feeling in regard to Roman Catholicism was
not of the intellectual order. He had intellectual difficulties, but the great moral difficulties were in the act
of melting away. Something was rising in him and
repeating to him that he would die a Catholic. Uneasy
about his future, he asked himself how he should know
where he would stand in two years? Where did Newman stand two years ago? Might it not be that he
would stand at the same point? *Strange thoughts visited
him*, according to his own expression. In his estimation, the theory of the Oxford school was in manifest
contradiction with the West and with the East. Anglicanism implied, on the one hand, principles that justified Protestantism and which Lutherans and Calvinists ·
were justified in invoking against it, principles, on the
other hand, which necessarily led to Catholicism. The
whole Anglo-Catholic movement rested also on a contradiction — there was question of Catholicizing the
Church, that is, as regards some of the faithful, of being
a means of grace for the supreme means of grace, of
bringing forth their mother, of making use of the individualist method of Protestantism in order to restore
Catholicism. In fine, despite these attempts at renovation, the Anglican establishment, mutilated, devastated,
ruined at the Reformation, remained incapable of offer-

ing an asylum to the penitent and a refuge to the disciples of Christ.

His diary, his letters to Robert Wilberforce and to
Mr. Gladstone, are filled with these sad avowals.   Yet
Manning, like Newman, whose intellectual temperament he did not possess, more than him, perhaps, would
have prolonged resistance to these doubts if he had to
give battle only to them.   He had a repugnance, an
invincible terror, at the thought of leaving his Church.
To him it was the one thing in the world, he wrote,
that most resembled death.   What a picture of the
condition of his soul in that letter to one of the confid-
ants of his anguish : All the bonds of birth, of blood,
of memory, of affection, of happiness, of interests, all
the seductions that can act on a will, attached him to
his present belief.   To doubt of it was to call in question all that was dear to him.   If he had to give it up,
it would be to him like death.

Fortunately there was going on in him, at the same
time, an internal, positive operation, that bore fruit in
his life and that was to give him the decisive impulse.
The Oxford school had given him a new conception of
the Church, perhaps the notion of unity; but it was
faith in the Holy Ghost, in his own office, in his constant action—in the Church as the source of infallibility, in souls as the cause of certitude—that was going
to complete this work, to reunite the *membra disjecta* of
this doctrine and to make of it a living religion.   Nothing is more striking than to show to what extent Manning, whilst he was waging this internal struggle and
whilst he still believed himself an Anglican, was already

a Catholic by instinct, at heart, in practice and in methods. He was so by his conception of the sacraments, by his celebration of the Eucharistic sacrifice, by his practice of confession.

Manning made his confession, sometimes to his assistant, Laprimaudaye, who preceded him into Catholicism, sometimes to other ecclesiastics. He heard the confessions of the faithful and professed that the sacrament of penance, far from being a counsel of perfection, as Robert Wilberforce had one day loosely insinuated, was a commandment so much the more strictly binding as sin abounds the more. A curious letter from him explains to Mrs. Sidney Herbert, the wife of the eminent statesman, his particular friend, his views on the delicate subject of the limit of the priest's and the husband's rights in the matter of confession and of the directing of conscience. Manning, like all the Anglo-Catholics of the time, violated to some extent the rules of the Church by taking hold of these usages. Confessions were made somewhat erroneously and perversely, without much care as to the limits of the parish and the rights of the diocesan. The legend, a legend in which undeniable testimony forbids me to put faith, relates that Manning, after he had become a Catholic and an archbishop, kept to this sad disdain for order and gave up usurping the rights of other bishops in the matter of confession and direction only on urgent representations being made to him.

All the same he had to some extent violated the wise practice of the Church, by preaching from the pulpit, in sermons addressed to all, precepts and instructions of conduct that the authentic director is very careful to model on characteristics and temperaments, to regulate in proportion to strength and to distribute individually. Mr. Gladstone, who wittily entreated his friend to open the compartment of casuistry, with which Manning's mind as well as his own was supplied, in order to discuss some delicate case of conscience, justly remonstrated with him that with the rules of life promulgated in one of his sermons a Member of Parliament, a Minister of State like him, would have nothing left for him to do but to give up his career.

Manning, moreover, was no less strict towards himself. He imposed upon himself, not only in Lent, but in every season, fixed hours for prayer, meditation, reading, and examination of conscience. He practised fasting, at least on Wednesday and Friday. He confined himself to reading the Bible kneeling, to reciting the Seven Penitential Psalms. He mortified himself by special acts of abstinence. From 1847 on, he gave up, for example, the luxury of horses and carriages. These were the beginnings of that asceticism in which he was to go so far later on. It will be acknowledged that this manner of living is not according to the Protestant spirit. Involuntarily did Manning show it by the customary use of formulas and expressions of the purest Catholicism. He spoke of the altar, of sacrifice; he promised to his friends commemorations *in sacro;* he wrote his private and confidential letters *sub sigillo confessionis.* Mr. Purcell, who is pleased to note trifles, points out that in 1847 Manning, while making use of a vocabulary thoroughly impregnated with Catholicism,

was still ignorant of the quasi-technical terms of Catholic devotion and improperly designated the Sacred
Heart and the Benediction of the Blessed Sacrament.
This trait simply proves to what point all this internal
development was spontaneous and personal.

Despite his constant progress in this direction, Manning did not find calm and joy. He accused himself
during those years, when he was called upon to play a
part in evidence on the stage of the metropolis and of
the Church, of worldliness and of ambition, of human
views and of cowardly compromises. This so-called
ambitious man was none the less troubled on that account by the offer of the post of sub-chaplain to the
Queen, which his brother-in-law, Samuel Wilberforce,
had just vacated to become a bishop, and which was
the first step in the ladder of dignities. He refused it,
after having sounded his conscience to the bottom and
examined his motives with a magnifying glass. He is
indeed the same man who, learning of the promotion
to the episcopate of a friend, who by that act betrayed
the cause of truth such as he had professed it until
then, and remained an Anglican by becoming a bishop,
thanked God for having spared him the trial of this
temptation.

God, in effect, was leading him by other ways. A
serious malady, which necessarily withdrew him from
his occupations and placed him face to face with death
and the eternal realities, in the spring of 1847, was to
him a spiritual renewal. He gave himself up to a
minute moral inquiry, he weighed his motives, his
actions, his thoughts, his prayers even, in the sanctuary

scales, and he devoted himself more completely to God. His secret diary of that period is a long and mystic conversation of his soul with Christ. He has himself dated from that crisis, during which he had also the sorrow of losing his mother, his conversion, formerly sketched under the influence of the Evangelical Miss Bevan.

The remarkable feature of this evolution is that the renewal of faith and piety in Manning was closely associated with his growing conviction of the truth of Catholicism. Why should we doubt that the appeal which he ever heard more pressing towards Rome came from Heaven itself, when he felt himself more and more in communion with Christ? He who detested controversy, who had pointed out to several souls that had entered on the same path as himself the danger of neglecting the elementary and sufficient means of grace, in his own Church, proudly seeking for a remote ecclesiastical idea, showed that, to his affected conscience, it was at the foot of the Chair of St. Peter and of the Vicar of Jesus Christ that the sources of eternal life sprang up. Henceforward, his Catholicism was no longer a temptation, it was a religion; it was no longer a theory, it was a reality; and the whole soul, no longer the reason or the mind alone, received its impress.

On leaving that long retreat, during which it appeared to him that God was severing him from everything in order to possess Him entire and to be His only possession, his physicians sent him to the Continent. There he spent the summer of 1847 and the first six months of 1848, especially in Rome. That journey was properly a course in ecclesiology and in practical Catholicism. Manning obeyed the principles of the Oxford school by haunting the Catholic churches on the Continent. The Tractarians, faithful to the theory according to which Anglicanism was a branch of the universal Church, would have deemed it equally culpable to frequent the Catholic *chapels* in England and not to frequent the edifices of that worship in France and Italy. Practice, however, hardly corresponded with this system. Newman, when he was converted, had never spoken a word to but two Catholic priests. Oakley, having entered a Catholic chapel by chance, had fled precipitately *in a panic of conscience.* Manning did not entertain such scruples. He betook himself assiduously to all the offices, he chatted with all the ecclesiastics, he visited all the monasteries. The effect on him of the ceremonies of worship was to confirm him in his secret Catholicism. These symbolic acts, this objective religion, that grand drama of the expiation and of salvation incessantly renewed and yet ever the same, all these things together seemed to him to bring out clearly the great realities of faith. In his estimation, Protestant worship was scarcely worthy of the name; sometimes, as in the cathedral of Basel, through which he passed, it presented, not an austere simplicity, but the dryness and nudity of a cold rationalism; sometimes, as in the Anglican churches, it presented to the faithful the body without the soul, the imitation of the forms without the vivifying dogma, of Catholicism. In St. Peter's, in the cathedral of Liège, in the basilica of Aix-la-Chapelle, in the *Portiuncula* of

Assisi, on the contrary, he felt himself at ease, at home, in close communion with the act and the priest.

In Rome he fully breathed the air of the Catholic metropolis. So as to occupy his leisure, he took in the spectacle of the beginnings of Pius IX., and of a revolution. He conversed with the men of the various parties, with Father Ventura and other members of religious orders. The Sovereign Pontiff granted him two audiences, on April 9 and May 11, the day of his departure. His diary of the time, so copious on everything else, mentions this fact in two lines. Fortunately the Cardinal made good the omissions of the Anglican. Pius IX., to whom, on behalf of his friend, Sidney Herbert, he presented a report on the famine in Ireland, spoke to him of Mrs. Fry, the prison reformer; in connection with this subject, of the Quakers; then, of the Anglican Church, of the observance of Sunday and of the saints' days; of communion under both species. In fine, he praised the good works that were being done in England in such large numbers, adding this somewhat Pelagian expression: "When men do good works, God gives His grace;" and, turning his gaze towards heaven, he closed with these words: "My poor prayers are offered every day for England." Thus ended that memorable interview between two men destined to exert together so great an influence on the Church and on the age.

Yet, scarcely had Manning returned to England when he plunged again into the thick of the fight. He found the Anglican world a prey to a violent agitation. Hampden had just been raised to the episcopate, that same Hampden whose appointment to the chair of theology at Oxford had formerly provoked a serious crisis. Manning had strongly declared himself in his letters against this choice. He surprised and scandalized some of his friends by the language of his Charge.   In it he adopted the bias of having recourse to an expedient purely formal, and refused, until a new order were issued, to see a heretic in a man whom the Church had not officially marked with this character.   Mr. Purcell finds in this act, in effect difficult to explain, a fresh example of Manning's slippery diplomacy. It may indeed be that the indefinite prolonging of this impossible dualism between the Catholic convictions and the Anglican position of the Archdeacon of Chichester exerted a demoralizing influence on him.   Perhaps we should see in it, however, only a scruple of legality and the natural repugnance of a man in whose estimation Anglicanism was altogether no longer hardly anything but a gigantic fiction, to make of an unfortunate prelate only the scape-goat of the general heresy.

  Nevertheless, this situation had its perils.   Manning was in a certain sense cut in half.   He was naturally exposed to contradicting himself.   When troubled souls addressed him, as formerly they had done Newman, in order to bring them back to the Anglican fold, his embarrassment was mortal.   To confide his own doubts to them, to initiate them into his secret struggles, would have been to exceed his right and to violate his secret. Compelled to keep them provisionally in the Church to which he still belonged, he was induced to use arguments of which he was not sure, and, when he had suc-

ceeded, it sometimes happened to him to have succeeded too well and to have turned away forever, in
spite of his ulterior efforts, a soul from the truth to
which he was himself to submit later on. Sometimes,
however, the truth gained the upper hand in spite of
all prudence, as when he answered a young Anglican
consulting him regarding the practical obligations of a
thoroughly Catholic state of soul : "The place for a
man who believes all the dogmas of the Catholic Church
is in the Catholic Church."

Action, however, to a man like Manning, has in itself such virtue, such seduction, such intoxication,
that he sometimes forgot, in the heat of a public discourse or of a particular conversation, not only, what
was already a very serious matter, his own thoughts
that he was holding in reserve, his own convictions, but,
what was still worse, the spiritual realities on which
they were founded. Another danger was, by reason of
practising *almosts* of the ritual, of devotion, of asceticism, that of blunting his religious sensibility and of
falling into that sort of clerical dilettantism that the
Anglican ritual of our day has become. I say so without meaning to make the slightest attack on the seriousness and the loyalty of men who courageously follow
their conscience; it does not suffice to play at Catholicism in order to feel its effects. A clergy without vocation, a service without consecration, an authority without legitimacy, a religion without reality, all that is
only the bark. The substance is elsewhere, and the
soul risks becoming weary by coming in contact with
these empty forms.

And so indeed a nature hungering after reality, action, truth, like Manning's, could not be satisfied forever with the hollow viands of Anglo-Catholicism. He began to feel that the very truths which he possessed, the half certitudes that retained him in Anglicanism, called for complementary truths, for the supplements of certitudes, and that, if he did not go to the end, he would lose even the little that he had. Christianity, in his estimation, implied Catholicism; to reject the latter systematically, would be to put himself systematically outside of the former. In other words, to him, as formerly to Newman, the question of the salvation of his soul began to gain the upper hand over that of the consistency of his doctrine and the coherence of his convictions. The purely intellectual problem was effaced: the religious, moral, vital problem presented itself more and more clearly. No longer would Manning have been able to give to others or to himself to hold humbly to the certainties common to all denominations, to practise merely the virtues that are not more peculiar to Catholicism than to Protestantism, to confine oneself to asking for those elementary graces that are the common patrimony of all souls in good faith. No longer would he have been able to repeat that it was not a question of life or death and that it was allowable for him to await a more precise vocation from on high. The internal work was completed. The cycle was run. External events were going to give the final impulse.

If I have insisted so much on this psychological evolution, it is not merely because of the interest that

is offered by the history of a soul, and of such a soul;
it is especially to answer Mr. Purcell's allegations and
those of certain of his critics, who have seen or have
wanted to see in this conversion, so tardy and so disputed, not the result of an unrelaxing struggle of six
years, the slowly ripened fruit of an admirable development of piety, but only the entirely political act of a
party man. If the statement that I have just made is
not the ample and sufficient refutation of this foolish
calumny, if there does not come out of it the distorted,
but the luminous and beneficent countenance of one of
the masters of the spiritual life grappling with the
dread problem of authority, I will have written in
vain. Not that I dream of disputing the part played
in Manning's final resolution by incidents like the
famous judgment in the case of the Rev. George C.
Gorham. All that I pretend is that, in regard to Manning as well as to Newman, the final impulse caused
only the determining of an act long since prepared by
an entirely internal evolution.

The Rev. G. C. Gorman was an ecclesiastic whose
ordination dated back to 1811, that is to say, to a period
of disciplinary and doctrinal laxity. After having received institution for the first time, without the least
difficulty, from the bishop of Exeter, he then saw himself refused it by this same prelate, in consequence of
an exchange of livings, because of his views on, or
rather against, baptismal regeneration. Gorham appealed from this refusal to the Court of Arches, the
ecclesiastical tribunal of the province of Canterbury.
Beaten in this instance, he carried his appeal before the

judiciary committee of the Privy Council, that is, before the last resort of English justice. It was a purely lay tribunal in law, since it was the Queen in her capacity of head of the State, and, consequently, according to the Protestant theory of the *summus episcopus*, of head of the Church, who there dispensed justice. The presence of three prelates as assessors, and purely by consultative title, in no respect changed the affair, so much the more as they were in the minority against the laymen. This court pronounced in favor of making provision for the Rev. G. C. Gorham. Two facts stood out clearly from this judgment with invincible evidence.

One is the royal supremacy. It was well known. Since the time of Henry VIII. and Elizabeth it was at the bottom of the English Reformation and of the Anglican establishment. Ordinarily, however, it was discreetly veiled. The whole Anglo-Catholic reaction had tacitly ignored it. People spoke of the Universal Church, of the councils, of the rule of faith; they systematically forgot that all these fine things were purely theoretical, and that in fact what was believed, what was professed, what ought to be believed and professed by the Church of England was what had been wished by Henry VIII., what had been instituted by Elizabeth, what was maintained by Victoria. The judgment of the Privy Council was a recall to the reality.

In the second place, this usurpation by the State, which had become the supreme judge of doctrine, did not remain a mere juridical fiction. It was exercised this time against the episcopal authority and in favor of a definite heresy. Not only was the Church severely warned that it was not its own mistress, or the mistress of its faith and of its discipline, but the true master declared that all that had been said, written, preached, for the past seventeen years, all Anglo-Catholicism, was a lie. It was allowable for an Anglican minister—for a priest, as the Tractarians said—to deny a sacrament, to teach and to practise Calvinism, nay even pure Zwinglianism.

It was too much for minds thoroughly penetrated with neo-Catholicism. There was great emotion. There was no longer question of knowing, as in 1845, whether the premises laid down by Newman permitted the refusal of obedience to the seat of unity, Rome. There was question of knowing whether, for one's salvation, one could remain in a Church that had become a purely human institution; whose faith, symbols, sacraments, discipline, recruiting, were at the mercy of the lay tribunals sitting in the name of the civil sovereignty. Mr. Gladstone, lying ill, sat up in bed to say to Manning that the Church of England was lost, unless it saved itself by some act of courage. At the last moment, the statesman receded before his own temerity. He refused, and he the thirteenth, at a meeting held at his house, to attach his name—because of his oath as a Privy Councillor—to the protest drawn up by Manning and signed by twelve faithful men and priests, among whom were Manning, Archdeacon Robert Wilberforce, Pusey, Mill, Professor of Hebrew at Cambridge, Henry Wilberforce, Keble and Hope Scott.

On March 19. 1850, in the library of Chichester cathedral, Manning presided at a meeting of the clergy

of his archdeaconry which adopted a shorter formula
of protest, but one no less clear. He drew up a declaration against the royal supremacy and had it signed by
eighteen hundred members of the clergy. Then, before
adopting the final resolutions, perhaps with the expec-
tation, against all probability, of a favorable solution at
the eleventh hour, he shut himself up in retreat. It
was, five years later, his Littlemore, the agony of his
Anglicanism. It lasted nine months, from March to
December, 1850. As he wrote about it to Robert
Wilberforce, every morning, on opening his eyes, his
heart was almost breaking. He felt himself divided
between truth and affection. Anglicanism, in his
estimation, was no longer but a ruin. Sometimes he
clearly discerned the port to which he was going:
Rome, the centre of the one, holy, visible, infallible
Church. On other occasions, vague visions floated before his eyes. If he remained an Anglican, he wound
end in being a mere mystic. God, he thought, is a
spirit, has no visible kingdom, Church or sacraments.
Nothing, in any case, would make him return to the
Anglican or any other form of Protestantism.

He conversed open-heartedly with Robert Wilberforce, who was passing through the same crisis. In
regard to the public, of those even of his friends who,
like Gladstone, could not conceive the sacrilegious idea
of leaving the national Church, he believed he could
remain silent as long as his party had not taken the
irrevocable step. Perhaps he still vaguely hoped
against all hope that the archbishops, in their quality
of spiritual heads, of patriarchs of Anglicanism, would

9

intervene to restore purity of faith. He had to give up this unaffected illusion when he saw the Archbishop of Canterbury, Sumner, refusing to receive a delegation, abstaining along with the entire episcopate, except four of its members, from the debate on the Bishop of London's bill transferring to the episcopal body the ecclesiastical jurisdiction in last resort of the Privy Council, and declaring that he would never lend himself to disputing the sentence of a regular tribunal and that he saw nothing unlawful in the admission to the care of souls of an ecclesiastic hostile to baptismal regeneration. This attitude was not altogether that of the Apostles proudly declaring to the Sanhedrin that it was better to obey God than men. Thus the Church was not merely reduced to slavery. It was so with the express consent of its heads, who were betraying it. It could no longer have but the name of Church. The reality had disappeared.

All Manning's friends, his brother-in-law, Samuel Wilberforce, the bishop of Oxford, whose two brothers were passing through the same crisis, Gladstone, Pusey, his relatives, his elder brother, who addressed letters of reproval to him and who always refused to see him again after his conversion, clearly felt that it was all over with him, that the rector of Lavington's submission to Rome was no longer but a matter of weeks, almost of days. Mr. Purcell, forgetting the documents that he himself has published, again seeks to convict him of duplicity. Manning, no doubt, was fulfilling the strict obligations of his charge, but his heart was at Rome. On November 17 he saw himself obliged to

convoke according to order and to preside over a meeting of the clergy of his archdeaconry in order to protest
against the Papal bull that had just restored, to the
great wrath of official Anglicanism and of popular
Protestantism, the Catholic hierarchy suppressed in
England since the accession of Elizabeth. The position
was an extraordinarily false one: he felt it, and he seized
that opportunity to acquaint his brethren in the ministry of the condition of his mind and of his formal resolve to abandon the Church of England.

The hour of final hesitations, of last combats, had
passed. Manning had given nothing to haste or to
passion. He had struggled as long as he had dared,
longer perhaps than a less scrupulous soul would have
done, against the voice of his conscience. Gradually
had he untied all the bonds which attached him to that
Church he had tenderly loved and faithfully served.
That time of retreat he had spent in reading the Brev-
iary, the initiation into those spiritual beauties of the
liturgy that had calmed and purified his soul. For the
last time he went and knelt by Mr. Gladstone's side, in
an Anglican church, in that little chapel of Buckingham Palace Road, in which preached an Anglican minister destined to become a Father of the Society of
Jesus, and, rising when the communion service began,
he said to his saddened companion that he could not
again communicate in the Church of England.

On April 6, 1851, the fifth Sunday of Lent or Passion
Sunday, Manning and his friend Hope Scott, who had
promised to walk hand in hand, made their abjuration,
their confession, their profession of faith, and received

conditional baptism and absolution at the hands of
Rev. Father Brownbill in the Hill street church. The
doubts that had tortured him until the opening of
Father Brownbill's door disappeared as if by magic.
A week later, on Palm Sunday, Cardinal Wiseman in
person confirmed them and gave communion to them
in his private chapel.

It was the end of a life. Manning believed that it
was even the end of his life, or at least of all public
activity for him. He had indeed, without the slightest
hesitation, resolved to get himself ordained as a priest;
but there his views stopped; he thought of living and
dying, in a tranquil and sweet obscurity, in the shadow
of the sanctuary. He had at last, after so many storms,
found peace, as is attested by this letter : "I feel that
I have no other desire to form than to persevere in what
God has given me for the love of His Son. What a
blessed outcome ! As the soul said to Dante : *E de
martirio venni a questa pace!*" The *Times* having expressed its belief in 1852 that it could announce his
return to Anglicanism, he wrote to it that he had found
in the Catholic Church all that he sought, nay more
than he would have been capable of conceiving, as long
as he was not in its bosom.

Manning was not one of those who turn back, or one
of those who, having once known and embraced the
truth, sleep in cowardly and egoist leisure.

PART THIRD.

I.

At the age of forty-three, after eighteen years in the ministry and eleven in the dignities of the Anglican Church, Manning again found himself alone, non-commissioned, despoiled, without office, without friends, almost without relations. In these painful experiences he thought he saw a warning from God against human attachments: he put himself on his guard against exclusive affections. Certainly it was not because the sources of love were dried up in that soul, in which we will see them later on playing rather abundantly until the evening of his life. Detached from purely human and terrestrial affections, he had not yet found in the practice of heroic or supernatural charity the use of his power to love. What dominated in him, however, was joy, a celestial joy, the cheerfulness of a soul inundated by the waves of grace, that at last has no obstacles.

His priestly vocation had not experienced the shadow of a hesitation. Less than six weeks after his abjuration, on Saturday, the vigil of the feast of the Holy

(133)

Trinity, Cardinal Wiseman ordained him with his own hands in his private chapel, and the second day after, on Monday, June 16, Manning, whom Father Faber, of the Oratory, had rapidly initiated into that ceremonial which, according to certain far from kindly judges, he never knew thoroughly, celebrated his first Mass in the church of the Jesuits and had Father de Ravignan as assistant at it. Though he already entertained views about him, the cardinal consented to let him go to study in Rome. There Pius IX. received him with these words coming from the heart: *Vi benedico con tutto il mio cuore in two egressu et in two ingressu*, treated him as a son, wanted to converse familiarly with him once a month, and placed him in the *Accademia dei Nobili Ecclesiastici*.

That sojourn in Rome, though there was something mortifying in a man of his age returning to school, going back, as he said, to the *nursing-bottle* and the *leading-strings* of the seminarian, like St. Ignatius before him, left a luminous trace in his life. Besides his studies and the privilege of his relations with the Pope, he formed close association there with the chief personages of the Curia, with the *Gesù*, with Father General Beckx, with the great theologian Perrone, and with Father Passaglia, who read the "Summa" of St. Thomas Aquinas along with him. At the end of three years Pius IX., who would have liked to keep him near himself, had to send him back in answer to Wiseman's reiterated entreaties.

The Cardinal Archbishop, in calling him to his assistance, was complying with a very just view of the

necessities of the situation. English Catholicism was
passing through a great crisis. For over two centuries
the object of a bloody, a most annoying persecution, in
the person of its priests, heroic rebels against the religion of Henry VIII. and Elizabeth, or of its laymen,
handed over, as victims of the Popish Plot, to the
monstrous lies of a *Titus Oates*, it had furnished innumerable martyrs to Protestant intolerance. It had not
merely endured those sufferings that bring with them
their compensation for exalted souls. Stricken with
civil and political disabilities, it had experienced what
is most cruel in persecution, namely, that shrinking,
that narrow-mindedness which persecution in the long
run brings about in the mind and heart of its victims.
The revocation of the Edict of Nantes or the revolutionary Terror gathers in the flower of a nation; it casts
it out or it shuts it up within, in a sort of home exile,
and of this choice set it makes a coterie infected with
the spirit of refuge or of emigration.

English Catholicism did not escape this law. Its
priests were the chaplains of a few great families. The
laity were disorganized, like the French Legitimists, in
a sort of home emigration. There were no middle
classes. The people comprised scarcely any but Irish
immigrants. In London the aristocracy frequented the
chapels of the Catholic legations and embassies; the
poorer quarters had only humble and mean mission
halls.

Elsewhere it was still worse. In Liverpool, four
chapels and fourteen priests for over a hundred thousand of the faithful. Four great events, which in a

certain sense marked the steps of a long evolution, came to change the face of things.

The French Revolution, by suppressing the colleges of Douay and St. Omer's, brought the younger clergy back to their natal soil in order to prepare them there for the priesthood, while at the same time the highly dignified example of the exiled French priests and the thoroughly new feeling of the solidarity of the Churches and of the aristocracies against the powers of destruction were weakening the Protestant and insular prejudice. The emancipation of the Irish Catholics in 1829, the breezy invasion of O'Connell and his *barbarians*, that is, of the democracy and of its methods, into the peaceful fold in which the *little flock* had browsed until then, without going outside, on rather unsavory grass, inaugurated a new era. There was an English Catholicism to which the disdainful tolerance accorded to an inoffensive minority no longer sufficed; it was conscious of the grandeur and of the strength of its principle; it carried the war into the camp of official Anglicanism or of militant Protestantism. Wiseman was its leader and its champion. At the same time the Oxford movement, by restoring Catholicism to a place of honor in the Anglican Church and by throwing Newman, Faber, Ward, Oakley, Dalgairns, Coffin, Manning and so many others into the Catholic Church, was transforming the moral atmosphere. A soil stricken with sterility for three centuries past was bearing new harvests, a dried stem was beginning to bloom again. Having become a conqueror once more, the Church raised her head. The new comers, excited by the

struggle, had not let their courage become debased into
cowardly idleness. No exotic blemish, no refugee tone
marked their conduct. They did not believe that the
conquest of truth, at the price of the most painful sacrifices, should exclude them from the arena of noble
combats.

Henceforward, in English Catholicism there were two
categories, two classes, two parties: the timid and the
valiant, the mute and the eloquent, the passive and the
active, the old and the new Catholics. If the division
was not always brought about in accordance with the
beginnings, if there were Catholics of the old stock
among the ardent and the converts,—one especially,
the greatest of all,—among the moderates this classifi-
cation was none the less correct on the whole. It was
natural that the former Protestants should in their new
Church be taken with all that had been wanting to
them in the old, present and visible authority, living
infallibility, ready and gladsome obedience. If all did
not go so far as Ward, who would have wished to receive every morning, along with his newspaper, at his
breakfast hour, a Papal encyclical containing dogmatic
definitions, they were all at least by vocation what it
has been agreed to call Ultramontanes. A conflict
with the semi-Gallicanism and the timid reserve of the
Catholics by birth was inevitable.

Pius IX. hastened it by restoring the ecclesiastical
hierarchy and by substituting for the apostolic vicari-
ates an archbishopric and twelve bishoprics. By proclaiming England ripe for return to the normal organism
of ecclesiastical life, the Apostolic Letter, "Universalis

Ecclesiæ," repudiated at the same time the chimerical hope of seeing the Anglican Church as a body, with its clergy and its prelates at its head, submitting to the Vicar of Jesus Christ. This act provoked an explosion of Protestant fanaticism in which Lord John Russell thought he ought to take part by having a law passed *ab irato*, destined to be tacitly abrogated even before it had been applied, prohibiting Catholic bishops from using territorial titles. In the bosom of the Church herself the offensive movement of propaganda and of conquest received a strong impulse from it. In the person of Wiseman, created a cardinal and appointed archbishop, the Holy See had a devoted lieutenant. Unfortunately, the episcopate counted too many members filled with the old spirit for perfect unity to be able to reign among the commanders.

The ten years that elapsed between Manning's return to London and his succession to the archiepiscopal throne were all filled up with sad struggles between the two opposing principles, still further complicated with deplorable questions of persons. Manning was necessarily mixed up in them by the nature of his opinions, by his temperament, and especially by the confidence of his archbishop.

From the beginning, out of obedience, he was destined to stir up many hostilities by founding a community of Oblates.

Cardinal Wiseman complained of not finding, in the numerical insufficiency of his clergy, the concurrence that he would have wished for from the regulars of his diocese. The quarrel between the diocesan authorities and the orders dated far back in England : had not Saint-Cyran, under the name of Petrus Aurelius, already to interfere in it? Manning's ideal, as was proved by his founding the congregation of the diocesan missionary priests of the Oblates of St. Charles, was not that of the Orders, entirely turned towards the perfection of the internal and contemplative life—even with the broad concessions made to practical life, and from outside, by the Institute of Ignatius of Loyola—it was that of the communities of secular priests living under a rule and in society, but with the view of serving as a reserve and, if we may dare say so, of *central brigades* under the head of the diocese.

It was to this creation that he applied himself without delay. Wiseman, who had successfully made use of him, during the Crimean war, in negotiating with the Government for the founding of a Catholic chaplaincy in the army, independent of the Anglican chaplain-general, could not yet place him at the head of a parish. He entrusted him with the creating of this congregation of auxiliaries, the need of which was so much the more pressing as it would be in vain, as he wrote, not without bitterness, to Father Faber, superior of the London Oratory, to appeal to the existing orders. Manning went to study at San Sepulcro, near Milan, the model institute of St. Charles Borromeo, and to submit to Rome the plan that he had drawn up. Cardinal Barnabò, head of the Congregation of the Propaganda, to which the affairs of England belonged, approved of it. The Pope sanctioned its statutes, with a special blessing, on January 21, 1857.

Three chief points constituted the essence of this rule : strict submission of the community to the head of the diocese ; amount of spiritual exercises and of theological studies fixed and calculated with a view to maintain at a certain level the spirit of the institution ; in fine, the absolutely secular character of the society, combined with the clergy of the diocese, and co-operating in its works.   Manning strove to bring out the immense riches of Catholicism by reason of this creation. He knew religious life in the cloister, the practice of the counsels of evangelical perfection, with its infinite shades, from pure contemplation and adoration to the manual and intellectual labor of the Benedictines and to the almost absolute suppression of the choir offices and the strict subordination of the exercises of worship to external activity as in the Society of Jesus.   He is in possession of those communities of priests intermediary between the atomic isolation of the secular clergy and the fixed grouping of the orders, those congregations without vows.   He at last lays in the secular clergy, in the simple priest, that corner-stone of the whole edifice, of the most marvelous instrument of propaganda, of moral influence and of hierarchical obedience.   What strength in this infinite variety!   What knowledge of the spiritual keyboard and of its innumerable touches!   And how one understands that Protestantism, even when most faithful to the spirit of the Reformation, sometimes tends to borrowing or to imitating these precious means of action.

On Pentecost Sunday, 1857, Manning was able to inaugurate his Institute.   Five priests and two clerics

—that was his whole force—were installed at Bayswater. Next day, at five o'clock in the morning, they went to celebrate their Mass in a neighboring church still in course of erection. Two thousand Catholics settled in the neighborhood, the church unfinished in which Mass was said on Sunday and once a week, a school with forty poor children—such were the beginnings of this work. For eight years Manning directed his congregation of the Oblates of St. Charles. He met with cruel trials there, there he waged fierce combats, there he endured severe defeats; none the less did he write of them in 1875 : "The eight years at St. Mary's have been the happiest of my life." His name had remained inscribed on the door of the little room into which the Cardinal Archbishop of Westminster loved sometimes to retire in order to taste there anew the delights of peace.

Peace! it was not peace, however, that marked this phase of his life. Side by side with the indefatigable activity that he displayed there, he had to wage combats without truce or let-up. His dear congregation of the Oblates of St. Charles was itself worth violent attacks to him. In the absence of regular seminaries, Cardinal Wiseman had thought he was doing well by confiding to him the direction of St. Edmund's College, in which the clergy of Westminster and those of Southwark were trained. He had reckoned without the head of this diocese, Rt. Rev. Dr. Grant, formerly his intimate friend, who had become his obstinate adversary. This prelate drew from the Westminster chapter a protest as vehement as his own, carried the matter to the

court of Rome, and there won his case on account of
some technicality. It was necessary to bow before this
decree.

The interference of the Westminster chapter was the
first symptom of an opposition that was to give way
only after a long struggle. For the moment Manning
bore the penalty of the early favors of Pius IX. When,
on April 8, 1857, six years to the day after his abjuration, he was appointed provost (or dean) of the chapter
of Westminster, this rapid promotion, which he as little
expected as did his new colleagues, carried their irritation to its height.

Thus raised to a rank already rather elevated in the
hierarchy, Manning, who saw in Wiseman the immediate representative of the Holy See, and who was con-
gratulating himself on being identified, like most of the
new converts, with this Cardinal's Ultramontane doctrines, was going to have to struggle against passionate
enmities. Convinced that this opposition was animated
by an *anti-Roman and anti-Papal* spirit and that there
would be no salvation for English Catholicism but when
*the present generation of bishops infected with Gallicanism
had passed away*, he was the Cardinal's right-hand man
in the painful struggles that occupy the closing years
of his episcopate. Wiseman had not many faithful
assistants in his immediate surroundings. There is
nothing more pathetic than the isolation of the closing
days of this great servant of the Church. His most
intimate companion, he to whom, in the gradual
weakening of his health and his inexperience of business, he entrusted the care of his practical interests,

Mgr. Searle, was a man without much delicacy, devoid of true affection, entirely devoted to the party of the old Catholics. This regrettable situation was partly the cause of the capital mistake that was to poison the end of that life.

The Cardinal Archbishop let himself be persuaded that he needed a coadjutor, and allowed his hand to be forced in the choice of this assistant so much the more important as he was to be invested with the right of succession. It was the Rt. Rev. Dr. Errington, bishop of Plymouth from 1851 to 1856, on this occasion created titular archbishop of Trebizond. Scarcely had the union been contracted when an absolute incompatibility of temperament was revealed between Cardinal Wiseman, ardent, bold, friendly to generous initiatives, the patron of the new Catholics and of their conquering zeal of neophytes, and Dr. Errington, the scion of an old race as proud of the purity of its blazonry as of that of its faith. Daily contact,—they were lodged together,—and the irritations of party spirit, were not slow in making this primitive want of sympathy degenerate into violent antipathy.

The tragic feature of this situation was that they saw no way out of it. Was Wiseman, as he was growing old, going to let authority gradually slip into the hands of Searle and Errington? If at that hour he had not a confidant, an energetic counsellor, he would have continued to groan over the evil without doing anything to remedy it. In this crisis, Manning was the Cardinal's support, his mainstay, perhaps his inspirer.

In his estimation there was question of a great and

decisive battle between error and truth, between consistent, logical Catholicism, faithful to its principles, and a bastard, emasculated Catholicism, adapted to the world and to the age. To a man like him, it was a sacred duty to give the strongest kind of helping hand to the cause of the Holy See, of unalloyed religion, compromised by the weakening of a prelate's health. There was going to be a future for the Church in England. There was question of knowing whether Wiseman's successor would continue or would destroy his work, whether he would appeal to the new forces or would return to the anti-Roman, anti-Papal, anti-Catholic Catholicism of old. As *procurator* or personal agent to the Cardinal, Manning negotiated for him at the court of Rome. He kept up a constant correspondence with the secret participating chamberlain to Pius IX., Mgr. George Talbot, who had the Pope's ear, whom a similarity of destiny and of convictions had bound to Manning, and who served as intermediary between the Sovereign Pontiff and those of his friends in England who wished to dispense with the official red tape of the Propaganda.

If Manning used this channel more freely than any-one else, Wiseman, who had appointed him his procurator with power to act, had only to congratulate himself on his zeal. Whilst the Cardinal, with the aid of fine petitions drawn up in good style, was rather gently carrying out his coadjutor's recall, Manning was working at it from 1859. Made a prothonotary apostolic with the title of Monsignore in the following year, he was gaining a foothold in that very special circle

which aids the Pope in governing the Church. In
England the crisis was becoming aggravated; nearly all
the bishops declared in favor of Errington; the secondary clergy indulged in indecent discussions even in
the Protestant and Liberal newspapers; the laity took
sides in a body with the champion of hereditary Catholicism, of sanctimonious somnolence, of the *dolce far
niente*.

It was the moment of dangerous transactions.
Wiseman, from weariness, gave way to it but too
much. Relieved by a Pontifical act in 1861 of the
assistance of a coadjutor who had become odious to
him, he attached less importance to the question of his
successorial rights on which everything turned, and
which, in reality and to Manning, was more important
than any other. And so indeed it was the agent with
power to act who eliminated these fatal compromises.
To the gloomy prophecies of schism made by Cardinal
Barnabò, prefect of the Propaganda, he answered with
full confidence in the effect of an act of authority.
Let Rome speak, he said, and everything will be well.
He was calmly convinced, he wrote, that it was one of
those *causæ majores* in which the Holy See is especially
guided by our Lord specially present. Such certainty
is not easily distinguishable from faith. It has its
moral quality, it gives out its full and pure sound.
And so indeed, in Manning, this Ultramontanism with
which he was so much reproached, very far from be-
longing to the domain of politics, even ecclesiastical,
and of the contingent, was the very fruit of his piety,
of his slowly elaborated convictions, of his religious

10

experiences. The man who was able to write these
lines, intended only for the eyes of a close confidential
friend—"The truth, the truth that alone has saved me,
is the infallibility of the Vicar of Jesus Christ, in so
much as being the only and perfect form of the infallibility of the Church, and consequently of full faith, of
full unity and of full obedience,"—that man could be
mistaken: he did not adopt these theories in order to
flatter a Sovereign Pontiff on whom his career depended.

With him, one could not repeat too often, Ultramontanism was only the last expression, the logical
outcome of a development of internal life and of piety
whose other fruits were an unfailing faith, an unbounded charity, and a rigorous personal asceticism.
Would it not be nesessary to complain of those whose
eyes would be shut by party spirit to that entirely
spiritual and religious origin of Manning's thoroughly
Roman Catholicism, or who would refuse to see in his
particular conception of Christianity the ever bubbling
source of that broad love of humanity and of that bold
view of the rights and of the duties of society with
which the latter part of his career was inspired?
Herein lies the very heart of our subject; let us, then,
say so once more, no matter how paradoxical the assertion may seem, that Manning's Ultramontanism was a
form of his piety, a step in his spiritual progress, and
it was in it that he found the inspiration of his Christian socialism, the motive of his popular activity, the
spring and the regulator of his generous temerities of
thought, of language and of conduct. It would be

absurd to force the note and to pretend to draw from
this fact general conclusions, but it is a fact that Manning was an Ultramontane to the same extent that he
was a great Christian, and that he was the apostle of
reforming Catholicism and of social reform to the same
extent that he was an Ultramontane.

Therein is the unity of his life. It is also the message of hope and of consolation that he wished to leave
to a generation weary of the negations of rationalism
and frightened at the problems of poverty and of evil.
To reconcile the two great opposing currents by making
them flow in one and the same channel, one of which
ended in the Vatican Council and in the proclamation
of the dogma of infallibility, whilst the other, after
having shaken or overthrown all the postulates of faith
and all the principles of certitude, came to beat with
its furious waves against the foundations of society
itself; to make of the Pope, proclaimed and acknowledged to be the incorruptible guardian of the deposit of
Christian revelation, the head of a Church that had
again become the refuge of the suffering and of the
oppressed ; to show to the people, disabused of the fictions of doctrinaire Liberalism, crushed under the weight
of the realities of economic Liberalism, the incomparable power of enfranchisement, of reparation and of
regeneration of a whole religion of liberty and of authority; in a word, to make of the gospel of Christ,
interpreted and applied by His Vicar and by the suc-
cessors of the Apostles, the charter of mankind ; to
make the Church kneel before the Cross and the world
before the Church, such was the plan that was gradually formed in Manning's mind.

He was not to be mistaken, in kind, in the confidence that he had placed in the Holy See. Undoubtedly, in the course of that struggle of six years, Cardinal Wiseman and his procurator endured some defeats. I have already spoken of that affair of St. Edmund's College, in which it was necessary to leave the place. On another point, the application of a new law relative to the registering of ecclesiastical foundations, Wiseman, who wanted to shun the danger of putting again in force legislation against mortmain property, won his case against the majority of the episcopate. On the contrary, he was worsted in the pretensions that he had raised as metropolitan over the inspection of diocesan colleges and seminaries.

All these differences did not fail to sour men's minds. Manning had to humiliate himself for a vehement scene that took place one day between him and Mgr. Searle, not far from Wiseman's sick bed. The Cardinal, who was sometimes irritated by the systematic hostility of men very far below him in merit, talent, character and services, as well as in hierarchical rank, apologized, by order of the Propaganda, for some rather malicious witticisms. In reality, Cardinal Barnabò, with that diplomatic obstinacy whose gentle resistance is almost invincible, favored Errington's cause. Fortunately the Propaganda at last refused to take part in an affair that was too delicate and too complicated. There was not question of issuing a judiciary decree, but of regulating an organic difference. And so, though the Holy Office had declared that there were no canonical reasons for deposing Dr. Errington from his *jus successionis*, Pius

IX., whose patience was almost exhausted, called up
the case, decided to strike what he himself called *un
colpo di Stato di Dominedio* and invited the Archbishop
of Trebizond to give up his rights. Errington obeyed.
He none the less kept a whole party that pretended
that his renunciation was of no avail and that specu-
lated on the early re-opening of the question of succession to Wiseman. There was only one way of warding
off this danger, namely, the nominating of a new coad-
jutator *cum jure successionis*. Manning adopted that
course which would have had, among other results,
that of shutting the door against the ambitions that
some attributed to him, if he had any. He worked
ardently to make the choice fall on the bishop of Birmingham, Dr. Ullathorne, who was far from being his
friend.

Fortunately, this combination ran up against an obstinate, invincible resistance : Wiseman had made trial
of a coadjutor, he had enough of it ; on no consideration did he want to begin the adventure over again.
It seemed that this long struggle was of little advantage to Manning. It had made for him irreconcilable
enemies in the episcopate, in the clergy, among the
laity, even in the outside Protestant and Liberal world.
It was the time when he was serving his painful apprenticeship in unpopularity. It is true that, in compensation, he had acquired valuable friendships in
Rome. Pius IX., in particular, had seen much of
him, had learned to know him, to place dependence
on him, to appreciate him. Mgr. George Talbot was
entirely devoted to his correspondent. These very

natural sympathies were to become still warmer by
reason of the great services that Manning rendered to
the cause of the Papacy.

With the same sincerity and the same passion as he
defended the spiritual authority of the Holy See, he
defended also its temporal authority. Napoleon III.'s
mad policy had just made the question of the temporal
power rise up in all its gravity. Italy had just been
organized with the military and diplomatic aid of
France. Founded in the name of that too famous principle of nationalities, set in honor by the head of the
only State perhaps that had nothing to expect and
everything to dread from it, the young subalpine kingdom stopped shuddering in the presence of the patrimony of St. Peter only at the *veto* of the conqueror of
Solferino, who had become the sentinel of the Vatican.
Whilst these contradictions were equally irritating Italians and partisans of legitimacy, vulgar Liberalism
allowed itself to reckon that the separation of the spiritual and the temporal required the subjection of the
head of a universal Church to the head of a particular
State.

Manning entered the lists in two series of conferences
which he collected into volumes, whose zeal people
began by praising at the Propaganda and which, a little
later on, came near being a bad business for him.
What was disconcerting was the infinitely more religious than political spirit of this champion of the Holy
See, who was protesting against all assimilation of the
sacred rights of the Pope with the terrestrial and contingent principle of legitimacy, and who was almost

condemning the use of material means and recourse to force in order to defend an entirely divine cause.

Non tali auxilio nec defensoribus istis.

The threat was made to put this rash work on the Index. Like Fénelon, he was quite ready to submit with a sort of bitter pleasure, happy, not at being put in the case of undergoing this judgment, but of having had the opportunity to give, in his time and in his country, an example of docility in a matter of opinion. This trial was spared to him. Some slight errors of form prevented neither the *Civilta Cattolica* from speaking favorably of his work, nor a new book by him on "The Glories of the Holy See at the Present Time," from meeting with a still warmer reception.

It was at this moment that came Cardinal Wiseman's death, so long expected and discounted. Recalled from Rome by telegraph, Manning had the consolation of bidding him adieu before closing his eyes, on February 15, 1865. The crisis was so much the more serious as great uncertainty prevailed on this occasion. Wiseman, cured of the taste for coadjutors by a single experience, had obstinately refused until the end to receive a new one. There was a party in existence that upheld Dr. Errington's indefectible right, in spite of his giving it up. There was question of knowing who would win, an adherent of the factional stationary old Catholicism, frightened at its own shadow, or one of the ardent, active, aggressive young Catholicism. Everything depended on the choice that Rome would make. The Westminster chapter had to present a list

of three candidates, on whom the bishops were to draw
up a confidential report. It seemed certain that, if
this body avoided offending the Pope by submitting
Errington's (the deposed coadjutor's) name to him,
and if they were sufficiently well advised to inscribe on
their list the name of the bishop of Birmingham, Ullathorne, the choice of this moderate, conciliatory prelate
would make no difficulty. The chapter were fore-
warned of the exclusion pronounced against Errington.
They took no account of it, and capped the climax of
their error by not finding a place for Dr. Ullathorne
along side of the ex-coadjutor, and the bishops of Clifton, Dr. Clifford, and of Southwark, Dr. Grant.

From that time the outcome of the crisis was becoming much more difficult to foresee. The English Government, entirely heretical and schismatic as it was,
thought it ought to interfere in favor of Grant, who was
looked upon favorably by the Ministers since his difficulties with Wiseman. Dr. Clifford none the less held
the string. If at Rome he was somewhat familiarly
called *un buon ragazzo*, his birth, his connections, his
temperament assured to him the devoted support of the
entire old Catholicism and of the leaders of rank in the
lay aristocracy. Cardinal Antonelli, a slave to State
reason, thoroughly steeped in politics, scarcely touched
by spiritual interests, was inclined to take great
account of the recommendations of the semi-official
British agent, Mr. Odo Russell; but the stamp of Lord
Palmerston and of Lord John Russell could not suffice
to make Dr. Grant's candidacy acceptable at the Vatican, where he was referred to as that *piccola testa e*

pettigola; of that prelate spoiled, according to Mgr. Talbot, by seventeen years' residence on the banks of the
Tiber, which had given him the taste for intrigue and
the duplicity of the Italian character without its noble
fidelity to the Holy See.

All that was deeply agitating the capital of Christendom in that spring of 1865. The cardinals of the Propaganda, with Barnabo at their head, hardly cared to
assume responsibility for an ungrateful task. In
reality, everything depended on the part that the Pope
would take in calling up the affair or letting it take its
course. An English member of a religious order, then
present in Rome, Father Coffin, openly wished for
what he wittily called, not a *coup d'état*, but a *colpo del
Spirito Santo*. Mgr. Talbot did not remain inactive.
Though Manning had pushed respect for the oath of
discretion that he had taken so far as to refuse to telegraph to him the names of those chosen by the chapter,
and though he had suspended his correspondence with
him for three weeks and more, at the critical moment,
from February 24 to March 18, the secret chamberlain
was kept sufficiently well informed by the provost himself, by Patterson, by Morris, to be in a position to
balance with Pius IX. the influence of the agents of
the Searles, the Erringtons, the Grants, the Cliffords
and the Ullathornes. If he assumed a little too much
prominence and attributed to himself more importance
than he possessed, if even for an instant he was so unaffectedly delighted as to believe that the Holy Father
had cast his eyes on him and to say so to his friend
Manning, he none the less had his use in his rank and
in his place.

Faint rumors were beginning to designate Manning. He had to undergo those alternatives of hope and of doubt that are so cruel to the ambitious. One day, he wrote bad news: If he said that not once had this perspective presented itself to his thought, he would be lying; but, while asserting that not for an instant had he thought it probable, or reasonable, or conceivable, he told only the strict truth. God knew that not once had his prayers expressed to Him the shadow of such a wish. . . The work on which he was engaged did not depend on the favor or the approbation of any one whomsoever, except our Lord or His Vicar. . . If the Holy Father ever wished for the destruction of his work, it would cease to exist before the setting of the sun: otherwise, no one in the world could destroy it . . . He had offended Protestants, Anglicans, Gallican Catholics, national Catholics, worldly Catholics, and the Government, and that public opinion which, in England, all day long and by every means, combated the Church and the Holy See. His correspondent knew whether that was the way that leads to rewards here below; he hoped to persevere in it until the end, sure that nothing dulls the edge of truth. What declaration of independence could surpass in nobleness and pride this profession of faith by a soul that set its dignity and found its liberty in obedience? Manning could wait with a firm foot for a decision that could change his destiny, but not the condition of his soul.

Pius IX., after having hesitated, after having spoken of the choice of Clifford as if it was to be made without him, had resolved, perhaps with the quite warm im-

pression of the *insulto al papa* which the presentation
of Errington's name amounted to in his estimation, to
interfere personally. He ordered special prayers and
Masses for a month in order to call down the light of
Heaven. The answer was not very long in coming. It
was the Pope himself who told Manning some weeks
later: *It was properly an inspiration that I obeyed in naming you. I incessantly heard a voice repeating to me: Name
him, name him!* This divine message Pius IX. did not
think he should resist. On April 30, 1865, he chose
Henry Edward Manning to succeed Cardinal Wiseman
as Archbishop of Westminster.

II.

On May 8, in the morning, Manning had just said
his Mass in the chapel of his community of St. Mary of
the Angels at Bayswater, when he received the official
scroll from the secretary of the Propaganda. His first
impulse was to go and kneel before the Blessed Sacrament. He was conscious of the crushing responsibilities that he was going to assume, but he had faith in
the aid of Him who had done all. His first thought
was for the portion of his new flock that clung closest
to his heart—the twenty thousand poor children of
London, still outside the action of the Church, for
whom he hoped to do something. His beginnings were
naturally marked by the spirit of conciliation : the
Archbishop of Westminster could extend his hand to
Provost Manning's adversaries. He was touched by
the eagerness shown in saluting his elevation by those
very men who should have most deplored it. The first

priest of the diocese to come to offer his congratulations to him was the vicar capitular, O'Neal, an opponent. The chapter, by its deference, hoped to make six years of bitter opposition be forgotten. Within two days, all the superiors of orders—except that of the Jesuits of Farm street, who permitted a few Fathers merely to make up for his abstention—all the heads of parishes, one hundred and ninety priests out of two hundred and fourteen, had come to pay homage to the new archbishop. The welcome was no less warm on the part of bishops: Dr. Ullathorne, whose name had been put forward for this great succession, wanted to be the first to congratulate his new metropolitan.

Manning's most ardent desire was to have himself consecrated in Rome by the Pope in person. He gave it up in order to make of his consecration the symbol and the pledge of that happy reconciliation. After a retreat in the Passionist convent at Highgate, he was consecrated on the Thursday of Pentecost week, June 8, 1865, fourteen years after his ordination. The ceremony took place in the pro-cathedral in Moorfields, Bishop Ullathorne, of Birmingham, officiating, and the assistants being Bishop Grant, of Southwark, and Bishop Clifford, of Clifton. Three hundred priests were crowded in the nave. When the new Archbishop was seen entering with the procession, with his spare form, his pale, almost transparent countenance, still further emaciated by a strict fast, an old Irish woman, lost in the crowd, exclaimed: "What a pity to take all this trouble for three weeks!" The end was not so near. Manning, who heard this exclamation, gave himself fifteen years of activity: God granted him more than twenty-five. Father Vaughan, Manning's friend and future successor, wrote to him that the burthen could not be heavier, but that there was no discouragement for the *apostle of the Holy Ghost* in England. Wiseman had finished his work a few years before his death. Manning's was to be, in his correspondent's thought, altogether more ecclesiastical and more spiritual. He was to give to England its St. Charles Borromeo and its St. Bartholomew de Martyribus. Manning felt himself quite strong with his motto, *Sentire cum Petro.* At Rome, in September, Pius IX. gave him the pallium and paternally recommended prudence to him.

There was nothing official in the relations between these two men. Pius IX. loved the archbishop tenderly, called him the man of Providence, entreated him to spare himself, to imitate that American prelate who had adopted as a rule never to do himself what a mere priest could do in his stead. As for Manning, outside of his convictions on the dogma of infallibility, he professed attachment mingled with veneration for the Pope's person. Mgr. Talbot having one day written to him that the Holy Father was a very good man, but, as he had said to him, he was not a saint, he had his weaknesses, Manning, who called Pius IX. the most supernatural personality that he had approached, replied that Mgr. Talbot knew very well that he had the idea that the Pope was a saint and that the *miserie umane* which one might discover in him were present quite as much in a St. Vincent Ferrier. If there was any exaggeration in this view, yet there was no flattery

mingled with it.   Manning's Ultramontanism was not
a borrowed doctrine, adopted in order that he might
stand well at court; it was the product not even of a
pure work of the mind, but of a slow elaborating of
conscience.   To this soul long tossed on the troubled
waves of Protestantism, it was at the very foot of the
rock of St. Peter—of that rock on which Christ Himself
had said that he would found His Church—that the
springs of certitude, of joy and of life had bubbled up.
It remains for me, while tracing Manning's episcopal
career, to show how that Ultramontanism, that strict
and absolute Catholicism, was the royal road by which
this precursor of a great movement went out to meet
modern mankind, its needs, its sufferings, and offered
to it the only efficacious remedy, the eternal Gospel.
In him breadth of action was in proportion to what his
adversaries called narrowness of doctrine.   By his example he showed the error of those who wish to lower,
to belittle Christianity, to despoil it of its supernatural
characteristics, so as to make it acceptable to the spirit
of the age.   The religion which he regarded as made
for a skeptical generation, suffering, overwhelmed, and
yet seized with its evil, on its guard against the pana-
ceas of charlatans, having gotten over the pompous and
misleading promises of the know-alls, proceeding, however, in accordance with the severe methods of science
and of criticism, is not a Christianity at a discount,
reduced to the level of a human system of morality or
of philosophy: it is the Christianity of the Apostles and
of the saints; it is the folly of the Cross, it is the scandal of the Gospel with its revelation and its miracles;

it is the Church, mistress of faith and subduer of errors. To Manning Catholicism, which will offer a refuge and a harbor to a generation tossed about on a shoreless and a bottomless ocean, weary of everything and especially of itself, is not a mitigated Catholicism, toned down, revised and corrected *ad usum Delphini*, reduced to the sonorous inanities of the "Génie du Christianisme," ready for all transactions with the State or with reason: it is the Catholicism of the great Popes and of the great monks; the Catholicism of unity, of authority, of infallibility; the Catholicism of Joseph de Maistre or of Lamennais in his early life. Mankind, according to a beautiful expression, is satisfied only by what exceeds it; it accepts only what is imposed on it; it bows only before what commands with authority. After all, it was never Christianity's method to address itself to reason only in order to convince it. It has always been necessary to rise above the region of the clouds, of doubts, of divisions, of misunderstandings, of storms; to mount on the summits of faith and of the divine certitudes in order to reach the zone of pure springs and vast horizons. Manning detested that lying breadth which, under the pretext of facilitating access to the city of God, destroys its ramparts and opens its gates to the enemy. In his estimation there were sacred narrownesses, attachments to unpopular causes, that are the very condition of true breadth.

Such is the deep reason for the species of dualism which people imagined they could detect in his episcopal career. There was no contradiction in that, especially nothing resembling the diplomacy of a Churchman

trying to redeem the excess of his devotedness to the
Papacy with the exaggeration of his advances to the
democracy of labor. The two parts of this life are connected like root and stem, like the tree and its fruit.
It was necessary in the first place to assert loudly an
uncompromising dogmatism, to make it triumph in the
Church, at the risk of getting mixed up, perhaps
irremediably, with opinion, before bringing to a sick
social organism the promises and the consolations of a
liberating Catholicism.

Already at that time the reëstablishment of unity in
Christendom was on the order of the day. The scandal
of those divisions with good reason preoccupied the disciples of the Master who said: *One flock, one shepherd.*

A society was formed in 1857 to work with prayer
for the restoration of unity. Side by side with two
hundred members of the Anglican clergy were found a
few Catholics more zealous than enlightened. The
Holy Office, consulted in 1864, had condemned the
theory dear to the advocates of a sort of federation of
the Churches, according to which there are three
branches of Christianity, namely, the Roman Church,
the Eastern Church, and the Anglican Church. A protest was addressed to Cardinal Wiseman, to the Holy
Father himself. Manning was not unaware that this
false idea of *corporate* reunion, that is, the negotiation
between equals of a sort of treaty between the Churches,
is often the chief obstacle to *individual* reunion, that is,
to submission pure and simple to lawful authority. As
a matter of fact, no matter with what sophisms the
edifying formulas of the champions of this bastard

federalism are masked, there are only two conceptions
possible, namely, that of the visible Church, one and
infallible, which required submission, and it is Catholicism;* that of the invisible Church never realizing
its unity externally, being satisfied with the mystic
communion of souls,—is that of Protestantism. Between these two there slips in the hybrid notion of
Anglicanism, which borrows from Protestantism its refusal to acknowledge the divine right of the centre of
unity and which takes from Catholicism its theory of
the Church in order to apply it, not without a manifest
usurpation, to the most insular, the most local, the
most dependent of the Churches. To these misplaced
pretensions Manning, who had had experience of them,
was pitiless. He declared most clearly that a single
soul won was worth more in his estimation than all
those clergymen so desirous of negotiating. The Pope
wrote, in a certain sense from his dictation, an answer
that did not even accord, from fear of encouraging
illusions, the title of Reverend to these ecclesiastics,
and Manning explained the Catholic doctrine in his
pastoral letter of 1866. In it he affirmed that there
was question, not of restoring the unity of the Church,
—there is only one Church, and Christ's promises have
guaranteed to it the indefectibility of its unity as well
as the immutability of its faith,—but of bringing back
to that Church, the only one worthy of the name, all

* The Encyclical, "Satis Cognitum," in reply to renewed attempts on the part of Anglicanism to have itself recognized as a
legitimate branch of the one and universal Church, has just defi-
nitively laid down the Catholic principles in the matter.

11

those who, by remaining separated from it, commit the sin of schism. This strictness very much displeased the Anglicans, especially Manning's former friends.

They did not understand this attitude in regard to a Church which Manning judged to be so much the more guilty as it was nearer to the light, and as its false semblances and its fine externals kept more souls far from the truth. Manning in this respect had come to prefer by far the condition of soul of the dissenting, purely Protestant sects to that of Anglo-Catholicism. He thought that the first sympathies of the Church ought to go *to those millions wandering here and there like sheep without a shepherd*, to those classes that form *the heart of the English nation, to those souls for whom Christ died, and who have been robbed of their inheritance by this Anglican schism* from which they lawfully separated themselves in their turn, and who, in spite of the prejudices of education, often show *more sincerity, candor and generosity in controversy* than the members of the Anglican Church. In these words there was a whole programme of action, admirably adapted to scandalize the Anglicans. Manning gave them a new grievance by his attitude in the grave question of the frequenting of the Oxford and Cambridge universities by Catholic youth. The suppression of the denominational character of these establishments,—the laicizing, to use the technical term,—seemed to authorize Catholic fathers of families not to deprive their children any longer of the double privilege of higher intellectual education and of participation in that university life which is the best apprenticeship for life in the world. Newman had not

ceased to have a sort of home-sickness for those places
where he had lived his happiest days and reigned as
absolute sovereign. Since the check of the plan of
founding a Catholic University in Dublin, he was living
a retired life in the Edgbaston Oratory, devoted to the
direction of a secondary school. There had been ✓
question of placing him again at Oxford at the head of
a house of his community, so as to exert a missionary
activity there, on the scene of his former glory. He
had even secured a tract of land for this purpose. The
project grew gradually. People dreamt of the establishment of a Catholic college affiliated with the University; Newman, shuddering with a quite natural
ardor, forgot that he himself, at Dublin, in 1851, had
forbidden Catholic youth to sojourn at the Protestant
universities. The adversaries of coëducation were in
commotion. They had attendance at the Protestant
universities condemned at Rome, and, even much more
severely, that at the laicized universities, by Catholic
youth. Manning had worked hard to obtain this de-✓
cree. Struck by the serious inconveniences of Newman's plan, but far from being in touch with the practical difficulties of such an undertaking, he was already
dreaming of the creation of that Catholic University
which he was to found at Kensington under the direction of Mgr. Capel, who was to bring him so much confusion, to cost him so dear—morally and pecuniarily—
and to end in so pitiful a check. For the moment,
this prohibition, in which Manning had so large a part,
was very deeply felt by Newman. From that time
dates the permanent coolness in the relations between

these two men, that famous broil on which it is so much the more important to have a clear explanation as Mr. Purcell's perfidious insinuations have the more disfigured its history, to the detriment of Manning.

For years already the two great converts had constantly been set in opposition to each other. Under a superficial analogy there was masked an almost absolute contrast of natures, of temperaments, of destinies. It was impossible for friends too zealous not to notice with some bitterness the change that had come about in the respective positions of Newman and of Manning since their abjuration. Previously, Newman was the king of Oxford, the oracle of Anglo-Catholicism; Manning was only an adjutant, a campaign ally. Afterwards, Newman lived in retreat, in a sort of disgrace, at the head of a college for young boys; Manning was the Archbishop of Westminster, the primate of England, the confidential close friend, the respected counsellor of the Pope. Such a difference in their lot must of itself alone be worth all favors to the one, to the other all the severities of opinion. Why should not this opinion have lavished its marks of kindness on the great mind, on the eminent writer, the honor of English letters, who passed for having drawn down upon himself the half disgrace in which he was vegetating by his courage in defending causes dear to the British nation? Why should it not have reserved its rigors for a man who seemed to take upon himself as a task to brave it by espousing the most unpopular causes, and whose rapid advancement people attributed to the gratitude of the Court of Rome? Anglicans, Protestants, Liberals them-

selves became easily affected over the great man who
saw himself rewarded for so many incomparable services done to the Church by a sort of ostracism. They
vaguely felt, in reality, that Newman had remained one
of them; that he had even been more so than since his
conversion ; that, Englishman as he was to the very
marrow of his bones, he had been thrown back towards
the half-way solutions of a sort of Anglican Gallicanism
since he had found himself in direct contact with the
realities of Catholicism. They were avenged, on the
other hand, for Manning's irreconcilable stand, for his
boldness in flinging at the public the defiance of his
defense of the temporal power and of infallibility, of
his aggressive and offensive Catholicism, by attributing
those convictions to ambition and his successes to intrigue. It was under this aspect that people then saw
him. Disraeli himself, who admired him sincerely and
who later on became connected with him, in the rather
too bright and highly-colored portrait that he has given
of him in his romance of "Lothair," rests on this trait
and makes of his Cardinal Grandison an improbable
alloy of asceticism and Machiavellianism. Friends
naturally were to spend their time in embittering the
quarrel. Newman, whether he would or not, was the
centre of opposition to all that was done at the Archbishop's House. Manning perhaps did not sufficiently
repress certain imprudent expressions used by those
around him. Occasions for conflict were not wanting:
the reunion of Christendom, University education, controversies relative to the Temporal Power, to the "Syl-
labus," to Infallibility. All these divergences, how-

over, would have left no traces, if there had been no
incompatibility of temperament between these two men.
I have already sketched these two physiognomies with
their essential differences : the man in his study, of
subtle thought, passed master in the most learned
mental tilting; the sworn enemy of rash generalizations
and of badly-defined assertions; in reality a skeptic by
nature like all intellectualists: the man of action, always
in the breach; neither having nor taking time to polish
his thought or to round his phrase, going straight to
the object, namely, the salvation of souls; liking to
proceed by massive and square assertions, hating deductions and argumentations. Newman was one of the
renovators of apologetics, a high-soaring dialectician; if
he fought a great deal and frequently humiliated reason,
he also liked it very much and often appealed to it.
Manning's idea was that the priest's mission is to give
testimony by his word, but especially by his life, to the
supernatural truths of Revelation.

These deep theoretical disagreements would not have
sufficed to bring these two champions of Catholicism
into conflict, without their characters receiving a shock.
If Manning was a man of authority, if he required of
his subordinates the loyal obedience that he practised
towards his superior, Newman had at last come to
losing to some extent the sense of reality in the artificial
atmosphere to which he confined himself. More than
ever the idol of a cenacle; always surrounded by pupils
who were to believe him on his word and by disciples
ready to swear *in verba magistri;* slightly intoxicated—
who would not have been so?—by the incense that

came to him from all directions and even from Protestants and Liberals, Newman was to see a certain dishonesty, explainable only by personal interest, in the condition of a mind in radical opposition to his own on everything, even when his steps were directed along the same way. Manning's elevation seemed to confirm this unjust view. Between the infallibilist Archbishop and the infallible Oratorian good relations were difficult. It follows, at least, from the letters published by Mr. Purcell, that Manning was ever the first to seek a reconciliation, the last to despair of it. He solicited Newman's presence at his consecration; the latter consented to come, but in the least gracious of answers. Each time that he had to address some congratulations to the Archbishop, he knew how, with somewhat of the art of the unfriendliness of devotees, to slip bittersweet epigrams into them. When at last Manning one day wanted, by a frank verbal explanation, to dissipate those painful misunderstandings, he ran up against a refusal, and he received from his old friend, whose hierarchical superior he was after all, an almost outrageous act of accusation. In it Newman declared his incurable distrust; he denounced in it a constant contradiction between the prelate's language and his conduct; he at last said forcibly that, every time that he had to do with the Archbishop of Westminster, he knew not whether he was on his head or on his heels. By thus forgetting charity and respect, the author of this demand exposed himself to a cruel rejoinder: had he not himself been constantly accused of Jesuitism, of casuistry and of duplicity, and had he not had to answer Kingsley's odious calumnies with his "Apologia?"[*] Manning did not reply exactly in this tone, but he had to turn some of his imputations back on his correspondent. This far from edifying dialogue was still kept up for some time, with long explanations by Manning, with short and sharp replies by Newman. It came to an end when, after the example of that prelate in "Le Lutrin," who dismisses the canons *aghast and blessed*, the illustrious Oratorian shot this Parthian arrow against his adversary: "In the meantime it is my purpose to say seven Masses for your intention, in the midst of the difficulties and anxieties of your ecclesiastical duties." Manning, though surprised, answered with tit for tat: "I am very much obliged for your amiable purpose of saying seven Masses for my intention, and it would give me great pleasure to celebrate one for yours, once a month, during the coming year."

This sacristy wheedling was, fortunately, not exactly the last word between two men of this character. After the accession of Leo XIII., when an effort was made to repair the long injustice of the Court of Rome towards the great athlete of the intellectual restoration of Cath-

---

[*] One day about that time the historian, Froude, said to a friend who had just published it in a volume of reminiscences: "The other day I met Newman walking in the park. Every movement which that man made, made me feel that one should not believe a single word he said." (A. K. H. B., "The Last Years of St. Andrews," 1890–1895, London, 1896.) This sally from the mouth of a man who had not merely been a disciple, but a friend of Newman's, is even more scandalous than unjust. It none the less indicates that there was an order of reproach which Newman should have taken good care to avoid against his neighbor.

olicism, the Archbishop of Westminster was not the last, nor the least zealous, in asking the cardinal's purple for the Edgbaston recluse. Unfortunately, a regrettable misunderstanding came near changing this natural occasion of reconciliation into a fresh reason for quarreling. Manning thought too hastily that the scruples of a man who did not dislike having himself entreated or laying down his conditions were a final refusal; Newman was more seriously wrong in seeing double-dealing on the part of the Archbishop in an error arising from the difficulty of deciphering the hieroglyphics of his subtle casuistry. It all ended in mutual explanation and understanding. Later on, the two cardinals who had come out of Anglicanism met twice in London. It is characteristic of these two men that, whilst Manning opened his arms to embrace the adversary who, with so sharp a rapier, had inflicted such penetrating blows upon him, Newman, having returned to the Edgbaston Oratory, found nothing but astonishment to express to his friends in regard to this fraternal embrace.

The Archbishop of Westminster, however, had found himself called to play a leading part in matters of great importance. The definition of the dogma of the Sovereign Pontiff's personal infallibility was in order. This story is still so close to us that it is difficult to write it with all the impartiality that it requires. Until the present time the great body of the public have perhaps looked at it through the stories of its adversaries. The opposition had, to a large extent, received its recruits from the camp of that Liberal Catholicism whose noble champions, the Montalemberts, the Gratrys, the Dupanloups, the Lacordaires, for such a good reason won over the sympathies of all generous minds. In France, no doubt, nearly all those who had combated the definition submitted, like docile children of the Church, in doing which, moreover, they had so much the less difficulty as, after all, they did only their elementary duty as Catholics, and as most of them had disputed only the opportuneness of this decision. ,

With many there none the less remained a sort of unfavorable prejudice against the chief promoters of the Council's decree. Two considerations, however, seem rather well adapted to weaken this impression. In the first place, the ulterior development of the destinies of Old Catholicism, that is to say, of that fraction of opponents, especially in Germany, who did not bow to the proclamation of the dogma, is scarcely of a nature to awaken very keen sympathies. If ever Church or sect rested with all its weight on the civil power, if ever nascent schism thought it could take advantage, not only of the favors of the State, but also of a persecution directed against the rival Church, as was the Kulturkampf, it was indeed Old Catholicism in Germany. In the clergy and among the laity of that little group there were highly respectable men: Dœllinger's name was of itself alone a watchword to it. It cannot be denied, however, that this pretended reform has miscarried,—or rather that it deserved to miscarry, —like all so-called spiritual movements that appeal to the secular power and that offer to it, in exchange for its protection, the services of a State religion. On the

other hand, the definition of the dogma of infallibility
by no means produced the result predicted by its adversaries. It might have appeared to a whole large
school, on the contrary, that there had been something
providential in this consummation of the work concen-
trating the spiritual authority in the hands of the Vicar
of Jesus Christ. On the eve of the events that were to
despoil the Holy See of its patrimony and to reduce
the Papacy to the condition of a purely ideal power, it
was not a matter of indifference that around the brow
of an old and feeble priest there should be the aureola
of a divine prerogative. And since then have we not
seen that power, moreover, so carefully surrounded by
guarantees and limitations by the constitution "De
Romano Pontifice," serve especially to the realizing of
the noble scheme that had been dreamt of by the
Liberal Catholics, that is to say, the adversaries of this
dogma? Did not Leo XIII.'s pontificate, thanks to
that great work of the pontificate of Pius IX., prepare
the way for the accomplishment of the ideal conceived
too early and especially followed up with too imperious
arrogance by Lamennais and the editors of the *Avenir?*
A Papacy sufficiently far removed above the region of
egoist interests, passions and rivalries to assume the
chief direction of the social reform movement, without
ceasing to be the keystone of the edifice of human society—a Church resting with sufficient solidity on the rock
of unity, sufficiently sure of its divine mandate to offer to
a suffering generation the remedy for all its ills—was it
not exactly what all these Catholics eager for reconciliation between Christianity and the spirit of the age were

ardently looking for? Whatever judgment one may
pass on the realization of this fine dream, the man who
clearly conceived the close solidarity between the two
parts of this programme—the man who wanted the
Papacy to be mistress in the Church and the Church
the servant of mankind—clearly merits that, in order
to appreciate his work, we should cut loose from party
spirit and from its prejudices.

Before, during and after the Council, Manning was
one of the most ardent champions of the definition.
He liked to recall the surname of " Diabolus Concilii "
which had been given to him by his adversaries. At
the jubilee of St. Peter, in 1867, being present in Rome
with five hundred and twenty of his colleagues, he had,
along with the bishop of Ratisbon, taken a vow to pro-
cure the proclamation of the dogma of infallibility and
to say special prayers to this effect every day. Though
the bull of convocation, dated September 13, 1868, did
not expressly state the question, the Archbishop of
Westminster none the less hurried to present to the
Pope two petitions in favor of the definition, emanating
from his diocese and signed by the chapter and by the
Oratory house at Brompton. During fourteen months
the preparations for those grand sessions which Christendom had not seen for three centuries, since the closing of the Council of Trent, excited Europe. The press
resounded with virulent controversies in which were
engaged especially the Augsburg *Gazette*, the *Civilta Cattolica* and the *Univers*, and in which the bishop of Orleans, Mgr. Dupanloup, took a most active part. Four
great committees of cardinals and of prelates, respect-

ively presided over by Their Eminences Bilio, Caterini, von Reisach and Bizzari, elaborated the *schemata* relative to dogma, to canon law, to mixed politico-religious questions and to regulars. The choice of the consulting theologians, called to assist the Fathers of the Council, was a serious matter. Mgr. Dupanloup wished in vain to have Newman as his. The English bishops had left him to one side, either because they had credited an improbable report according to which the Pope wanted to have recourse directly to his lights, or because his opposition to the dogma of infallibility had put him in too bad odor at Rome. The struggle became strangely animated, obstinate, and of still doubtful issue. Döllinger was not satisfied with having recourse to the lawful weapons of theology, of erudition, nor even with denouncing the triumph of the Jesuits, by reproaching Manning with the zeal of a convert. He entertained no scruple as to making an appeal to the civil power and as to claiming, in the name of a so-called Liberalism and in the interest of the principles of modern society, the resurrection of the *veto* by the crowned heads. The German bishops, in the address which they adopted at Fulda, placed themselves on the more circumscribed ground of the inopportuneness of the definition. Mgr. Maret published his great work, beneath whose learned and ponderous dissertations some thought they discerned the menace of interference by that Liberal Catholic party which had just come into power in France with the Ollivier-Daru ministry. Mgr. Dupanloup never tired in eloquent protests. Manning had issued a pastoral letter on the burning subject.

He was very clearly accused of heresy by the bishop of Orleans; and it was necessary to answer this passionate controversialist, who did not know English, that he had condemned a mistake made by the French translator.

The hour for the opening of the Council was approaching; Manning set out on his journey. At Paris he saw M. Thiers, who made to him the professions of faith of the most edifying deism and naively said to him: *Do not make life too hard for us! Do not condemn the principles of '89!* M. Guizot declared that *the temporal power was the last pillar of European order,* and that he saw in the Council *the only moral power capable of restoring peace to the world.* The first business of this assembly was the electing of the deputations or committees on which the episcopate of each nationality counted one or several representatives. It was not on Manning, but on Grant, that the choice of the English bishops fell. The Italians made up for this by electing the Archbishop of Westminster. To trace in detail the history of the Vatican Council does not enter into my plan. I must be satisfied with characterizing Manning's part in it. That part was threefold: within, among his colleagues, in the preparatory labors and the general discussions; without, close to the Pope and close to the witty and distinguished agent whom England kept without accrediting him at Rome. His activity was immense. It was equal to that of his great adversary, Mgr. Dupanloup, whom he was astounded to see sending off packages of manuscript every day. With both of them it was a matter of conscience: if the one declared that he would *shed tears of blood at the thought of*

all the souls that would be lost by an inopportune definition,
the other sincerely believed that the salvation of the
Church and of the world depended on the promulgation
of this truth. Inside the Council Manning struggled
energetically, at first to have signed and to present the
postulatum or the proposition that was to place the
question on the order of the day, then to obtain a
favorable report from the delegation *de postulatis* or initiative committee, and afterwards to get rid of the
motions for adjournment or the amendments and to
get a vote on the real issue. On this ground he displayed all the qualities that would have made of him
a parliamentarian of the highest order. At the same
time, as good judges tell us, he showed himself the
prince of diplomatists. The familiar access that was accorded to him by Pius IX.'s paternal kindness assured
to him valuable advantage which he took no care not
to use. He had the privilege of entering by a hidden
stairway and by a secret door leading to the Pope's
apartments in the Vatican, and he has himself described the stupefaction of the diplomatists or of the
ecclesiastics who were patiently waiting their turn for
an audience in the Sovereign Pontiff's antechambers,
on seeing this visitor leave whom they had not seen
entering. He made use of this privilege on several
occasions in order to bring energetic counsels to the
Pope or to provoke decisive steps; he had never turned
it to more useful advantage than on the day when,
having learned that Doellinger, to whom the opposition
had given the *schema* of the constitution, was preparing
to drive the government of the king of Bavaria to take

the initiative in a previous intervention of the powers,
he ran to ask the Holy Father to relieve him from his
oath of secrecy, in order to be able to communicate to
Mr. Odo Russell the true state of affairs, and to put him
at the same time in a position to prevent the Gladstone
Cabinet from reaching an unfortunate decision.

It was in his relations with Mr. Odo Russell that
Manning especially gave proof of the qualities that
would have made of him an ambassador or an eminent
statesman.   He had formed close relations with this
lordly diplomatist who for ten years filled with distinc-
tion at Rome a mission that had no official character.
Thoroughly Whig and Protestant as he was, Lord John
Russell's nephew had acquired a passionate taste for
the Eternal City, wished only to prolong his sojourn
there, and had become a convinced advocate of the
maintenance of the temporal power and of the definition of the dogma of infallibility.   Such a condition of
mind in Her Britannic Majesty's representative made the
cultivating of his acquaintance valuable.   Besides the
interviews and conversations of the week, every Saturday, the day on which the Council held no session, the
Archbishop and the diplomatist agreed to meet in order
to take a long stroll on foot in the Campagna.   There
the conversation touched on everything, from the great
eternal problems to those trifles that formed the pasture
of what Louis Veuillot called the *gossipings of the Council.*
Manning there said to his chatting companion, and
through him to Lord Clarendon or to Gladstone, all
that he could and ought to say to them.   It was a fine
success for him to make himself a docile and safe in-

strument of the diplomatist who was later on, at Berlin,
to play at close range, and not on such unequal terms,
with that rude adversary who was called Bismarck.
The devouring activity of the opposition was doomed
to failure from the moment that the governments in
which it had placed its hope held aloof. In the British
Cabinet all the credit that Mr. Odo Russell enjoyed
with his chief, Lord Clarendon, was required in order
to counterbalance in Mr. Gladstone's mind the influence of the advice given by Sir John Acton,* Dœllinger's friend and the great leader of the newspaper
campaign in England and in Germany, who energetically supported the proposal that the Munich Cabinet
interfere. France, at first tempted to make Napoleon
III. play the part of heir to Louis XIV., by reviving
the *veto* of the crowned heads, was absorbed in the
grave concerns of the plebiscite and of foreign politics.
In vain did the minority become obstinate, keep up a
menacing agitation outside, within practise a sort of
obstruction, exhaust all the means of adjournment,
make parade of the probable figure of its votes,—which
it estimated at between a hundred and forty and a
hundred and fifty, by adding the *juxta modums* to the
non placets,—try, in fine, to intimidate the minority by
exalting the moral force of an opposition more than
half made up of the bishops of France and of Germany
and recruited from among the glories of the Church.
In the debates it did not appear that this superiority, a

---

* Now Lord Acton, lately a member of the Gladstone-Rosebery
Cabinet from 1892 to 1895 and appointed to the chair of modern
history in Cambridge in succession to Sir John Seeley.

12

little too sure of itself, shone undisputed. Cardinal Bilio ranked the discourse delivered by the Archbishop of Westminster, in the general discussion, as on an equality with the harangues of the Strossmayers and the Dupanloups. Manning himself finely said: "They were wise: we were fools. Well! strange though it be, it has happened that the wise had been always wrong and the fools always right." Events came hurriedly. Disappointed in the hope of interference by the civil power, and beaten on their proposal to prorogue the Council *sine die*, the opposing bishops left Rome or decided to hold aloof. On May 14, 1870, the general discussion had been opened on the *schema de Romano Pontifice*. On July 13 a majority of four hundred and fifty-one votes against eighty-eight *non placets* and sixty-two *placet juxta modums* adopted in general congregation the chapter on Papal infallibility and the immediate jurisdiction of the Holy See. The Pope, entreated by a delegation from the minority to interfere in favor of conciliation, did not think he could comply with this wish. Five days later the Council held its fourth session and ratified its preceding vote by five hundred and thirty-three *placets* against two *non placets*.

Next day, July 19, war was declared between France and Germany. In the whirlwind of those tragic events, the peculiarly religious question seemed relegated to the rear. One might believe that Providence had allowed the Papacy to reach the last degree of a slow evolution only to reprecipitate it from the highest eminence into the abyss: *ut lapsu graviore ruat*. The Italian troops, docilely attached to the talons of the victorious Prussians, entered Rome on September 20 through the far from glorious breach of the *Porta Pia*. Was it the end of the spiritual authority at the same time as of the temporal power of the Holy See? Was it the chastisement for the proclamation of infallibility? Manning did not believe anything of the kind. While maintaining the protest of violated right against the sacrilegious usurpation of the patrimony of St. Peter, he saw in a trice that a new era was opening, in which the Papacy, despoiled of its temporal domains, reduced to its mere spiritual prerogative, was going to become the arbiter of peoples and kings, if it knew how to use its royal poverty and its ideal power. In his estimation the definition of the dogma of infallibility on the eve of that brutal invasion was providential in the highest degree. Perhaps, in the closing years of his life, when his ideas were fully ripened and when his hatred of the fatal alliances between earthly causes, contingent principles, like that of legitimacy, and the cause of God and His Church, was strengthened, one would not have to press him very hard in order to make him acknowledge that the destruction of the temporal power had in it also something providential. Not that he dreamt of impossible and dishonoring transactions between the Vatican and the Quirinal, or that he wavered in the imprescriptible claim of the necessary sovereignty of the head of the Catholic Church. Certainly it was not in the Archbishop of Westminster,—convert as he was, by the virile practice of the regime of poverty and of the independence of a Church entirely separated from the State, with the doctrine of pure and simple liberty, as in England and in America,—it was not in him that one ought to look for an advocate of those bastard concordats that would reduce the common Father of the faithful to the role of chaplain of the House of Savoy. A devoted son, a faithful friend of that Pius IX., who rewarded him with so much zeal by raising him to the cardinalate in 1875 and from whom he had the consolation of receiving a tender adieu, *Addio, carissimo*, on his death bed, before piously closing his eyes, Manning would have thought he was betraying his benefactor and his own past by lending himself to the squinting diplomacy of those great conciliators who would sacrifice all the rights of conscience to a smile from the powerful ones of this world.

His feeling was quite different. He has expressed it in his secret diary, in which he equally repudiates the two schools, both of which lead to the spiritual as well as the temporal abdication of the Papacy, the one by feigning to count on a miracle, the other by preaching inaction as the most sacred of duties. We ought to know, he exclaimed as far back as 1876, whether we ought to shut ourselves up in a new ark like Noë, or should not rather, like all the Pontiffs since Leo the Great, act on the world. And he added that the parable of the lost sheep suffices to settle the question. So this time again the source of Manning's politics, the secret of the evolution that was going to make of the champion of the temporal power and of infallibility, in the latter part of his career, the apostle of the reforming Papacy and of social Catholicism, must be sought in the depths of a truly priestly conscience and in the ardent desire of saving souls.

This noble conception of the Papacy liberating itself by liberating the Church, conquering the world by force of serving it, was the inspiration of the last twenty years of this life. Naturally it led Manning farther outside of the purely ecclesiastical domain. There, however, he still waged fierce combats. The most formidable adversary with whom he had to cross swords was Mr. Gladstone, who took advantage of his return to private life in 1874 to uphold, in his "Vaticanism" and other pamphlets, that it was impossible for Catholics, by accepting the dogma of infallibility, to observe a loyal allegiance to their sovereign. It was at a great sacrifice that Manning threw himself into this controversy which again interrupted for fifteen years a friendship that of old had already been suspended by his conversion and gradually renewed since 1865. No more than was customary did he keep aloof from this painful duty. It was indeed the same juvenile zeal that he continued to exercise in the administration of his diocese and in the conduct of his spiritual functions, particularly in preaching, in the directing of consciences and in the education of the clergy, so dear to his heart. If his journeys to Rome became a little less frequent, it must especially be attributed to the progress of the age. Made a cardinal in 1875, he knew how to wear the purple with a simple dignity that further enhanced its splendor. Ascetic in regard to himself, he followed a regimen of absolute frugality and drank only water,*

* The Cardinal had become an abstainer from being merely tem-

but he continued to show to others a hospitality without display, yet in conformity with his rank. In England all the hostilities of the beginning had not been disarmed; more than one hatred of the devotees was smouldering under the ashes; but the hostile voices had become silent; his authority among Catholics was almost equal to his popularity among outsiders. In Rome, though he suffered from pointing out a certain decadence there, a certain contraction of mind, he was always a power. He was seen there, not only under Pius IX., but, after this Pontiff's death, at the conclave in which an assembly of Italian cardinals, among whom figured Their Eminences Franchi, Bilio, Bartolini, Monaco and Nina, offered the tiara in all sincerity to the Archbishop of Westminster, and in which he was one of the chief promoters and authors of the election of Cardinal Pecci. This simple fact is quite injurious to the legend of antagonism between Leo XIII. and Manning. If there was not between them the unique friendship that bound the latter to Pius IX., the new Pope was careful to lavish on the Cardinal-Archbishop of Westminster, at the time of the journey that he made *ad limina apostolorum* after his accession, the marks of

---

perate. When one day at a temperance gathering he said: "I drink wine only on my doctor's orders," a voice called out to him: "Change your doctor." He did so. When on another occasion, without giving his name, he was urging an Irish laborer whom he met in the street to "sign the pledge" (to drink no more), and when he added by way of argument: "I have signed it," the man he was conversing with, who had recognized him at once, overflowing with humor like all his countrymen, said to him with a twinkle in his eye: "Oh, sir, no doubt you needed it!"

well-merited confidence and deference, and to follow
his advice about persons and things in England. It
suffices to recall the part that was taken by Manning
in the triumph of Cardinal Gibbons' ideas before the
supreme tribunal to which they had been referred, and
to point out the thorough agreement between Leo
XIII.'s great encyclicals and all the religious and social conceptions of the Archbishop of Westminster, in
order to refute these foolish inventions.

III.

Manning, as soon as the Vatican Council had realized
his ecclesiastical programme, was able, without fear of
being attacked from behind or of seeing the earth open
under his feet, to follow out the realization of his social
programme. He had quite naturally been led to this
order of concerns by the exercise of a charity that had
brought him into contact with all the sufferings of our
time. In those frightful resorts of the East End of
London he had learned to know that wretchedness of
which material poverty and the lack of everything are
only one of the traits, and not the worst; which is de-
graded by the conditions of its existence, to which the
very excess of its needs precludes the hope of rising to
the surface, and which is made criminal in spite of
itself by the infamy of the circumstances to which it is
subjected. He had gone down to the bottom of that
hell compared with which that of Dante is a sojourn of
the blessed. There he had met that hero of Protestant
charity, Lord Shaftesbury. One tastes the purest and
highest of joys on seeing these two great Christians,

placed at the antipodes of thought and of life, the one a Cardinal Archbishop of the holy Roman and Ultramontane Church, the other an uncompromising Protestant overflowing with Biblical indignation against the *great prostitute of Babylon*, shake hands and commune together in the name of that love of mankind out of / which the religion of Christ has made charity. Both of them conservative by origin, by position, by instinct, by intellect, both of them by contact with those realities contracted a socialism *sui generis* against which the demonstrations of political economy lose their force, are powerless. No one is ignorant of the glorious part taken by Lord Shaftesbury in legislation for the protection of children and of labor. It remains for me to say what Manning's activity was in this order.

His disposition, and circumstances also, had long kept him apart, after his abjuration, from undenominational associations. In 1871 he was called to sit in the committee that had been organized at the Mansion House to come to the aid of the needs of Paris, after the siege. It was his beginning. From that time on there was scarcely a philanthropic work or one for the improvement of morals, outside the domain in which the rival Churches display their flags, in which the Archbishop of Westminster was not a born member. It was a curious and instructive spectacle to see the reception given, the rank accorded to this prince of the Church of Rome in a thoroughly Protestant country and one in which the law, even only yesterday as it were, recognized the Catholic priest only to brand him with civil and political incapacity. Personally, Man-

ning scarcely cared for these homages: he attached
value to them only by reason of establishing precedents
for fixing the position of his successor or bringing the
condition of his colleagues into prominence. So far
did he carry this feeling of solidarity that, later on,
when the last barriers in his way had been removed,
and when he was invited to the Court or to the Prince
of Wales', he accepted these amiable attentions of the
Queen or of the heir to the throne only in so far as
they were not addressed to him personally, exception-
ally, but to his dignity, and when his brethren of the
episcopate could take advantage of them. Another
very serious innovation was the calling of this Cardinal
Archbishop to sit on several of those royal commissions
to which the English Government likes to entrust in-
quiries on subjects of public interest. Manning took
part with the Prince of Wales in that which so profoundly studied the question of workingmen's lodgings,
and he exerted a powerful influence on it. The
Queen's Ministers also had recourse to his enlighten-
ment in the matter of legislation against intemperance.
From all these supererogatory tasks which presented
themselves he did not think that he was free to hold
aloof, in the first place and especially because of their
intrinsic utility, then also with a view to the manifest
triumph that his mere presence in these official bodies
assured to the principles of toleration. His heart, however, was less in these labors, which in a certain sense
belong to the administrative order, than in his own
works of relief and assistance.

It cannot be too often asserted, because it answers

certain doctrinal statements according to which theoretical devotedness to social reform would always be in inverse ratio to practical activity for the comforting of wretchedness: it was by the royal road of charity; it was by carrying out the fundamental precept of the Gospel; it was by following as closely as possible in the footsteps of Jesus Christ that Manning reached that broad and bold view of the evils of our society and of the best manner of remedying them. The first work to which he devoted himself was that of temperance. He had seen with his own eyes and touched with his own hands the effects of alcoholism, perhaps the greatest scourge of our civilization: the family destroyed; children the innocent heirs of all the ills of body and soul and victims of abandonment or of bad treatment; drinkers the slaves of a pitiless tyrant, gradually ruined in their health, disgusted with work, forgetting the way to the workshop and that to the church; in short, hell upon earth, in the heart of our great cities. In the presence of such a state of things Manning was not a man to fold his arms. He not only appealed to all the resources of religion—it was always the best of his forces in that holy crusade—he had recourse to every means of action, to association, to enthusiasm, to everything that awakens the conscience and strengthens it, to everything that moves and stirs the popular soul. He founded, he propagated the League of the Cross. He wore his cardinal's robes on the platforms of public assemblies. In the beginning, and for a long time, he found only repugnance and hostility in the ranks of the clergy and of the pious laity. His resolutely modern and popular methods frightened the wise and the reasonable, and were revolting to the delicate. He was reproached with borrowing something of his noisy means of propaganda from that Salvation Army for which, moreover, within the limits prescribed by his impeccable orthodoxy, he openly professed keen sympathy. Some had a grudge against him for making himself too familiar with his Leaguers, especially with those tried lieutenants out of whom he had formed *the Cardinal's bodyguard.* His annual feast of the League of the Cross at the Crystal Palace, with that quasi-military organization, those banners, those bands of music, those distinctive ribbons, that sort of review held by the commander-in-chief, that prince of the Church haranguing the multitude, those frenzied acclamations, all that troubled and roused to indignation those well-fed and ponderous Pharisees whose horizon never extended beyond the walls of a sacristy. Nay more: some grave doctors expressed doubts regarding the perfect doctrinal correctness of a movement that seemed to give to temperance, to abstinence even, a disproportioned place in the catalogue of the theological virtues.

Manning let them talk. *Si hominibus placerem, non essem servus Dei:* This was his whole answer to these critics. He went on his way, giving all his spare moments to this propaganda: even during several years—truly dangerous excesses—his brief summer vacations; practising abstinence himself; making himself accessible at every hour to his staff, or even to the first repentant drinker who came to ask him for aid and advice. Such zeal must have its reward. Gradually, in proportion

as the work grew, objections disappeared. The secular
priests in hundreds, the religious orders in bodies, became associated in this activity. The League of the
Cross multiplied its branches over the entire surface of
the country, and counted its members by tens of thousands. The Cardinal's bodyguards were fourteen hundred. Children were enrolled in large numbers. One
day, in the presence of death, Manning could write:
*One of my greatest joys is that I have saved many poor
drunkards.*

The second branch of his activity to which it is meet
to call attention here is that which has reference to
childhood. This ever had the first claim on him.
When he was made Archbishop, his first impulse was
to think joyfully of all that he was going to be able to
do for those poor children deprived of the succors of
the Church, the number of whom in his diocese he
estimated at twenty thousand. We know how, to the
great indignation of those Christians who prefer a monument of cut stone to an edifice of living souls, Manning, who had begun by buying a vast tract of land,
did not feel himself obliged to bring to completion the
building of the cathedral planned and begun by Wiseman, but was satisfied with the temporary pro-cathedral, while directing all his efforts and that of the
donors to the education of the children.* It was the

---

* Manning allowed the poor children of the neighborhood to
make a garden for their play out of the enclosure intended for the
building of the future cathedral. As for the Archbishop's House,
which he purchased and in which his successor still resides, it was
an immense bare barracks, built to serve as a club house for the

time when England, under the Gladstone ministry and
under the direction of Mr. Forster, adopted that great
system of popular education which was to give so powerful an impulse to the diffusion of light, but which
laid down in an urgent and acute form the question of
religious instruction. Opinion had not yet reached the
point at which it could lay hold of this great truth, that
liberty of conscience and the rights of parents are none
the less injured by a public education, distributed in
the name of the State and at the expense of the tax-
payers, from which the name of God and religion are
banished, than by a system of denominational education
imposed on all. It was necessary, then, to maintain and
even to develop the denominational schools, especially
for a minority like the Catholics; it was furthermore
necessary to found and to support at great expense
orphanages, industrial schools, houses of reformatory
training for thousands of children who, in non-Catholic
establishments, would have risked losing their faith.
That was Manning's work, and it was colossal. The
proof that he succeeded in it is, in the first place, the
spectacle of those large and handsome diocesan and
parish schools.* Then it is the important part which

non-commissioned officers of the regiment of the Guards. He was
attracted by the size and the austere simplicity of the place, where
he *camped* until the end.

*In 1891 there were 3,204 Catholic children in the orphanages,
the Public Aid schools, etc., of London, all subject to the periodical
surveillance of a diocesan inspector; 2,253 children in charitable
asylums, and 22,580 other children in the Catholic free schools of
the diocese.

the Archbishop of Westminster played in the great commission of inquiry on primary education, in which he was truly the inspirer of the conclusions of the report in favor of amending the law of 1870. In the last place, it is the plan that he proposed to the House of Commons, then deferred from its regular order with the promise of being taken up next year, and in which Cardinal Vaughan and his suffragans, in spite of many defects, welcome a sincere effort to give satisfaction to the claims of the Church.

Manning, moreover, did not confine himself to this somewhat professional activity. The man who said that *a child's tear not wiped away cries to God as loudly as blood spilt on the ground*, was the born patron of all works of protection, of saving and of defence for childhood. He coöperated in particular, and with unparalleled zeal, with the great undenominational society founded and directed by a dissenting pastor, the Rev. Benjamin Waugh, to prevent and suppress cruelty to children. When the editor of the *Pall Mall Gazette* undertook his campaign against criminal sensuality and its attacks on minors, Mr. Stead had no more intrepid aider and abettor than the Cardinal Archbishop, who went so far in his generosity as not to disavow publicly the pranks into which an indiscreet zeal dragged his protégé. This way of committing himself to any one who showed that he was animated with a truly generous spirit and seemed disposed to serve mankind, greatly scandalized some of those around Manning. Those who imagined that they could give him a lesson on the danger of these acquaintances did not return to the attack; the priest, the prelate, the prince arose and relegated them to the place which they should not have left.

Yet all this activity could not fail to bear all its fruits in a mind like Manning's, accessible to the end to the teachings of experience. In politics his starting point had been that of a Conservative pure and simple, of a straight-laced Tory. As long as he remained an Anglican, he remained faithful to that party. He looked at all questions from the standpoint of the national Church. Ecclesiasticism to some extent stifled in him Christianity and its inspirations. All that was changed after his conversion. He was no longer a member of the *Church of England*, but of the *Church in England*. To him the civil power was no longer the natural-born protector, at the same time as the regulator, of the spiritual power. With the logic of his mind, it did not take him long thoroughly to modify his conclusions on all points. He called himself a *Mosaic radical*, a disciple of Moses, so as to indicate at the same time the fundamental conservatism of those advanced opinions and their Biblical origin. It was not the first time that the Old Testament was responsible for a transformation of this sort: did not Voltaire say irreverently of a prophet whose freedom of speech the Socialists of our day would scarcely equal: *"That way Amos is capable of anything?"*

Among the new opinions which Manning drew from his new religion, we ought to place his love for Ireland in the first rank. He began by venerating in her the Island of Saints and the Land of Martyrs, watered by

the blood which England, associating the spirit of persecution with that of domination, has made to flow in
torrents there.   Though he had denounced Fenianism,
as well as all secret societies, as a sin, it did not take
him long, in his daily relations, intimate and familiar
with a race that formed the immense majority of his
flock, to entertain towards it that affection, at the
same time enthusiastic and compassionate, which the
Irish have never failed to inspire in those who know
them.   He was the first among Englishmen to adopt
in his conscience the idea of Home Rule, that is, of
limited autonomy, as the solution of a perhaps unsolvable problem.   When, in 1886, Gladstone rallied to a
policy that he had honestly combated as long as he had
been able to believe in the success of the only alternative acceptable to a Liberal, that is, of the realization
of a programme of organic reforms, Manning came close
to his old friend, between whom and himself there had
been a coolness since their controversy on Vaticanism.
The Irish of the large cities adored him.   On the
annual feast day in honor of St. Patrick, whom he had
made the patron of a *drinkers' truce*, intended to snatch
some victims from alcoholism, the Archbishop's name
was received with loud applause.   The day on which
he celebrated the silver jubilee or twenty-fifth anniversary of his episcopate, all the Irish Nationalist Members of Parliament, Protestants and Catholics alike,
with Parnell, a heretic, at their head, went to the
Archbishop's House to offer him their congratulations.
This proceeding was a subject of affliction to all those
Catholics,—and they are numerous in England as

elsewhere,—who have not known how to distinguish the cause of God and of the Church from that of social order, from political conservatism and from legitimacy. It is true that, in his later years, Manning gave them so many causes for scandal that one more was scarcely important. Willingly would they have set down these pranks of the Cardinal to the account of age and the isolation in which he was ever more and more confining himself; but Manning's vigorous appearance when he officiated, the brilliancy of his eagle look, the majesty of his bearing, the indefatigable sprightliness of his mind forbade those perfidious allusions to apoplexy of the Archbishop of Grenada. The Cardinal, in fact, reserved a much more disagreeable surprise for his detractors. In the closing years of his life he was going to preach by word and act that doctrine of Catholic socialism, or rather of social Catholicism, which is indeed the most hateful of the novelties that can excite the wrath of those of the faithful accustomed to see in the Church the guardian of their interests and in religion the best safeguard of property.

Novelties? I am in error, for one of Manning's merits was precisely to throw new light on the teaching of Catholicism on these essential points, and to borrow from St. Thomas Aquinas, whose wisdom enlightened by revelation is no more defective on this chapter than on the others, the fruitful principles of a social science that is not vitiated by the materialism of its premises and by the partiality of its deductions. I can give only a very light sketch of the many and remarkable writings which the Cardinal devoted to this subject, either

13

in the form of articles in the great reviews, or of controversial letters in the columns of the *Times*, or even in that of pastoral letters. His theory rested on a few very simple general ideas. To him political economy was a moral science, and the conclusions of the abstract study of wealth had no value but in so much as they were subordinate to the universal laws of conscience. In his estimation labor, too long relegated to the rear and deprived of the protection of which it stood so urgently in need, ought to be treated on the same footing as capital had been. The only economic unity, the essential social quality, was man, the human individual, with his physical and moral needs, his aspirations, his rights. The end of society was by no means the production of wealth, but the acquiring of the greatest possible happiness for the greatest number under the empire of the moral law. Among the social axioms there was none more chimerical, according to him, than to promulgate the pretended dogma of "let alone" or of the non-interference of the State. The whole economic history of mankind had consisted in violating this so-called principle, it is true, especially to the advantage of the capitalists. In our time, the labor-protecting legislation to which Lord Shaftesbury has so gloriously attached his name, had begun to restore equilibrium. Manning deemed it so much the more deplorable to stop in this course under the pretext of a worship to be paid to the fictions of a certain political economy, as there was still an enormous amount of work to be done in this direction and as justice is no less interested than the security of society in the continuance of this undertaking.

Since 1873 Manning had been inspired with these ideas that were so much the bolder at that date, as German *pulpit socialism* had hardly begun to accord its patronage to the founding of Trades Unions among agricultural laborers by Joseph Arch. A conference that he gave in 1877, on the rights and dignity of labor, contained the explanations of these principles. In it he sketched that social organization, the presentiment of which was haunting him and which, in many of its characteristics, partakes of the nature of the guilds of former times. While utterly repudiating sympathy with revolutionary ideas, therein he clearly concluded in favor of fixing by law the normal duration of a day's work and, after having pictured some of the effects of unlimited competition and of the unbridled play of supply and demand, he closed with the declaration that these things cannot—they should not—last. The piling up of enormous wealth like mountains, in the hands of certain classes, or of certain individuals, must continue indefinitely unless a remedy is applied to the condition of the people. Society cannot rest on such foundations. In a pastoral letter of 1880 he pointed out the existence, in the heart of our great cities, not of poverty, which is an honorable condition, but of pauperism, which is its corruption and the degradation of the poor; and he painted in the darkest colors those inequalities of our social condition, those abysses dug between classes, those abrupt contrasts between those whose lot is luxury and those whose destiny is wretchedness. In his articles in the *Contemporary*, the *Fortnightly Review*, the *Nineteenth Century*, in his letters to

the *Times*, he receded neither from bold thoughts nor
from rash words.   His *right to steal*, grafted on the right
to work and to assistance, though in reality borrowed
from the most orthodox theology of the Church, was
well calculated, no doubt with premeditation, to startle
every economist.   Besides, none the more did Manning
recoil from compromising relations than from ideas
that were looked at unfavorably.   The famous American socialist, Henry George, the leaders of the new
trades-unionism, the Tom Manns, the Ben Tilletts, the
John Burnses, received a cordial welcome at the Archbishop's House.   This house had become the meeting
place, not only of the clergy and of the faithful of his
diocese, but of a multitude of dreamers, agitators, reformers, nay even revolutionists, who, having come on
the first occasion as visitors, sometimes returned as
penitents.   Manning, through his League of the Cross,
through his relations with the Irish, had come in direct
contact with the people, with the laboring classes.   It
was in that direction that he wanted the Church to
turn.   He felt that for him to seek to lean on governments or on the directing classes, was to court cruel
disillusions.   When Pope Leo XIII. sent a special
delegate, Mgr. Persico, to study the question of the
Plan of Campaign and of the land agitation in Ireland,
the Archbishop of Westminster regretted that he had
entered into communication with the Ministers and
the landlords instead of going direct to the people
and of consulting the Nationalist M. P.'s, the patriotic
clergy and the bishops.   With all his power at Rome
he supported the cause of Archbishop Gibbons, of Bal-

timore, when the latter was accused of favoring Socialism and of being too indulgent to the Knights of Labor.
In fine and especially, he exerted a decisive influence
in the great strike on the London Docks in the months
of August and September, 1889.

That episode in the war between labor and capital
was of great importance. It was the mobilizing of the
lower layer of the laboring classes, of that unskilled
labor which had remained until then outside the ranks
of trades-unionism. With these elements, there was
reason to fear that, in the London atmosphere over-
charged with electricity, the strike might degenerate
into a genuine civil war. Fortunately the dock laborers had level-headed men for their leaders, Burns,
Mann, Tillett, and they obeyed them with admirable
discipline. It was only sixteen days after the beginning of the struggle that the Cardinal was called upon
to unite his efforts with those of the men who were trying to bring about conciliation. In an interview with
the directors he entreated them to yield on the question of salary in the name of their interests, of the
imminence of a revolution, and especially of the sufferings of the poor. A committee was formed with the
Lord Mayor as chairman, on which sat the Cardinal,
the Anglican bishop of London, who very soon repudiated responsibilities that were too heavy for him, Mr.
Sidney Buxton and some others. It was on Manning
and Buxton that the whole weight of the negotiations
fell. Convinced of the justice of the chief claims made
by the strikers, they exerted themselves with rare
energy to obtain liberal concessions from the managers.

A compromise was suggested: the laborers were to obtain the amount of wages that they asked,—the famous *tanner*, or twelve cents an hour; but the new tariff was to go into effect only on March 1, 1890, that is, after a delay of six months. Burns and Tillett declared that it would be impossible to accept such a long wait for their comrades; Manning exerted himself strenuously to obtain the date of January 1 from the directors. It was the final limit of their concessions.   There was question of getting the transaction sanctioned by the strikers, who were already accusing their leaders of treason. The Cardinal, accompanied by Mr. Buxton, betook himself to the Dockers' headquarters, in the favorite Poplar district.   A meeting was held in the school hall of the Catholic church in Kirby street. The audience were boisterous. All those strikers were for the first time tasting the fruits of solidarity. They believed that they were sure of victory. To ask them to wait for more than three months for the clear and full result of those weeks of privations and sacrifices, was to appeal to reason against instinct in beings who were in their first movement. On the other hand, the Cardinal, thoroughly satisfied as he was of the justice of their cause, knew that therein lay the only means of making it triumph, and that the directors were looking only for an excuse to recall their concessions. For nearly five hours—from five until ten o'clock in the evening—that old man of eighty-three, that prince of the Church, pleaded with familiar and impassioned eloquence in the interest of the laborers and of their families. In closing he drew tears from the driest eyes by making an eloquent appeal to their love for their wives and children. His cause was won. The emotion was intense among those simple and rough men. One of them thought he saw the Madonna hanging over the orator's venerable head, giving a sign of approval. The real miracle was the conquest of those simple minds and of those rough hearts by that old priest who never served Christ better than by procuring peace on that occasion.

It is on this closing scene that it is proper to leave Manning. There no longer remained to him but a few months to live. The shadows of evening were falling ever more thickly on his path. His health was too feeble to allow him to leave his residence in order to betake himself to that Athenæum Club, where he was so fond of recreating himself in the society of a Ruskin, a Bryce, a Gladstone, or even of some Anglican prelate. Though surrounded by the love of the whole people, by the veneration of his Church, by some faithful affections, he felt himself isolated. His thoughts were naturally turning back towards the past. He gave himself up to a prolonged examination of conscience. He again passed over the course of his long life. He gave thanks to God for having revealed to him the plenitude of His truth. He humiliated himself for his errors and his faults. He enumerated to himself, when he felt discouraged by the comparison of his career with that of a Shaftesbury, of a Gladstone or of a Macaulay, the five great truths to which it had been given to him to do homage: the unity of the Church, the rule of divine faith, the infallibility of the Church and of its head, the office of the Holy Ghost, the tem-

poral power of the Vicar of Jesus Christ—and also the
three great causes to which he had devoted himself:
the religious education of children, temperance, and the
education of the clergy. A weariness of living was
coming over him, but, at least, the fear of death never
visited him. There are men, he said, who do not like to
speak of their end. As for him, he liked to do so, as it
aids in preparing oneself and it takes away all sorrow
and all fright. It is a good thing to be filled with the
thought of the light and beauty of the world beyond
the grave. That is what inspired St. Paul with his
desire to rove. This simple, candid, radiant faith was
indeed the feeling that was to accompany and facilitate
that great Christian's death. For nearly two years he
serenely saw his weakness increase. In the beginning
of the year 1892 he understood that the last hour had
struck. After an illness of six days, he received the
last sacraments and made his solemn profession of faith
in the presence of the Westminster chapter, on January
13. During his last night he was watched by three
friends, namely, Bishop Vaughan, his successor; Canon
Johnson, his secretary, and Dr. Gasquet, his physician.
At dawn on the 14th, whilst Bishop Vaughan was saying Mass for him in his oratory, the soul of Henry
Edward Manning, Cardinal Archbishop of Westminster,
was called back to its God.

Almost at the same time there died a young prince
in the direct line of succession to the throne of England,
the Duke of Clarence. This national mourning did
not detract from the great outburst of sorrow that accompanied the disappearance of this octogenarian.

One would have said that the London of the laborer,
of the people, of the poor, felt itself orphaned. In the
multitude that defiled in close ranks into the mortuary
chapel in which were exposed the mortal remains of
the Archbishop, clad in the Cardinal's purple, were to
be seen, alongside of his colleagues in the episcopate,
of the members of his clergy, of the laity of his flock,
of the neophytes whom he had brought into the Church,
of the penitents whose director he was, of the friends
whom he received, with his customary good grace, and
of the individualities of every sort, of every opinion and
of every origin, who had tasted his generous and toler-
ant hospitality, an anonymous multitude, in part de-
cently clad, partly haggard and raggy, that had come
to see for the last time the emaciated features of the
patron of the poor, of the people's Cardinal. His
funeral took place on January 21st at the Brompton
Oratory. In that vast sanctuary were assembled to pay
the last honors to him all the representatives of the
Church, of the aristocracy, of politics, of the directing
classes. It was outside that the most imposing manifestation took place. The streets were filled with
dense masses of people. The League of the Cross with
its banners, the Irish National League, the Temperance
Alliance of the United Kingdom, the London Trades
Unions, the dock laborers' societies, the Good Templars,
the Bands of Mercy, groups of children, religious con-
fraternities, political associations, workingmen's corpo-
rations, the grand army of toilers, and, behind, in still
closer files, that other great army of the wretched who
ordinarily come out into the light only in the dark

hours or trouble and storm—that variegated multitude formed the hedge along the march from the Oratory to the cemetery.   At several points bands of music played funeral marches.   When the coffin passed, all that multitude, Catholics and Protestants, socialists and revolutionists, knelt or bowed.   One would have said that, for one day, over that casket in which slept a great servant of Christ, the two worlds, between which our materialist and mercantile civilization has dug an abyss, extended their hands to each other weeping and were reconciled in a common mourning.

Such were the obsequies of Henry Edward Manning, cardinal priest of the holy Roman Church, of the title of Sts. Gregory and Andrew on Mt. Cœlius, Archbishop of Westminster, primate of England.   Our age has no doubt seen more pompous: it has seen none more affecting.   It was truly a whole people that was partaking in them.   Manning needs no other funeral oration.

I have tried to tell the story of his life: that long effort in the direction of truth, that heroic sacrifice of all that is dear to man, that passion for certitude which cast him at the feet of the infallible Church and, in that Church, at the feet of the Vicar of Jesus Christ, the incorruptible guardian of the deposit of faith.   I have tried to tell also of that noble attempt to bring mankind to the Church, and to give to the Church consciousness of its mission of enfranchisement, of consolation and of salvation for society as well as for the individual.   In the presence of that grand figure, made up of austerity and of love, of asceticism and of charity, in the presence of the memory of that man who loved power, but only to devote it to the noblest of uses, the word that involuntarily rises to the lips to sum up all that history is that of Scripture : *Ecce sacerdos magnus;* his was truly the soul of a priest.

INDEX.

Bilio. Cardinal, 173, 178, 179, 182.
Birmingham, Newman at Oratory near, 70, 152, 156.
Bismarck and Odo Russell, 177.
Bizzari, Cardinal, 173.
Blomfield, Bishop, on Manning, 110.
Bristol, English Church Union at, 66.
"British Critic," 105.
British Isles, the Church in the, 91.
Brompton Oratory, 172, 201.
Brotherhood of Christ, 43.
Brownbill, Rev. Father, 132.
Buckingham Palace Road Chapel, 131.
Bull, Anglican theologian, 91.
Bunsen and the Jerusalem bishopric, 105.
Burgon, Dean, 15.
Burns, John, 196, 197, 198.
Buxton, Sidney, 197, 198.
Bryce, James, 199.
Byron at Oxford, 83.
Byronism, 87.

Calvinism, 128.
Calvinist biographer of Manning, 4; Calvinists, 115.
Cam, the, 83.
Cambridge, 128; University's rivalry with Oxford, 82, 83; Catholics and, 162, 177.
Campagna, Roman, 176.
Canterbury, 126, 130.
Capel, Mgr., 163.
Cardinals, College of, 35; do., English since Reformation, 34.
Carlyle, Froude's life of, 3, 80.
Caterini, Cardinal, 173.
Catholic antiquity, 22.
Catholic ceremonies, 65.
Catholic chaplain in the army, 139.
Catholic Church, 27, 57, 63, 65, 67, 113, 124, 179.

Catholic Emancipation, 33, 96.
Catholic evolution, 61.
Catholic historian, 19.
Catholic, Manning's life as a, 29, 133–203.
Catholic peoples and Protestant peoples, 17.
Catholic system, living unity of the, 50, 65, 102.
Catholic University in Dublin, 163; Kensington, 163.
Catholicism, 9, 12, 15, 17, 32, 37, 38, 40, 42, 44, 45, 48, 49, 62, 63, 67, 70, 72, 76, 85, 86, 90, 91, 98, 101, 103, 107, 109, 114, 115, 118, 120, 121, 124, 125, 135, 136, 137, 140, 142, 144, 145, 146, 147, 151, 152, 158, 159, 160, 161, 165, 180, 193.
Catholicizing dilettantism, 18.
Catholicizing evolution, 41.
Catholics, two classes of, in England, 137, 154.
Chair of Peter, 113, 120.
Charles I. and Parliament, 91.
Chelsea, sage of, 80.
Chichester, Archdeacon of, 49, 107, 110, 123, 128; diocese of, not Oxford, 106.
Chinese Wall, 47.
Christ, 68; brotherhood of, 43.
Christendom, 61, 65, 153, 160, 165, 172.
Christian life, ideal of, 62.
"Christian Remembrancer," 111.
Christian skeptic, Newman as a, 38.
Christian socialism, 42.
"Christian Year," Keble's, 97.
Christians, 60; and philosophers, 57.
Christianity, 10, 15, 17, 38, 41, 42, 44, 45, 50, 56, 62, 64, 67, 68, 92, 146, 158, 159, 160.
Church and State, Gladstone on, 107.
Church, the, 27, 28, 44, 45, 46,

www.ingramcontent.com/pod-product-compliance
Lightning Source LLC
Chambersburg PA
CBHW020608030726
47497CB00007B/2134